Princess Plume

Dean Lombardo

www.cleanreads.com

PRINCESS PLUME
Copyright © 2016 DEAN LOMBARDO
ISBN 978-1-62135-556-4
Cover Art Designed by AM DESIGNS STUDIO

This is a work of fiction. Names, places, characters, and events are fictitious in every regard. Any similarities to actual events and persons, living or dead, are purely coincidental. Any trademarks, service marks, product names, or named features are assumed to be the property of their respective owners, and are used only for reference. There is no implied endorsement if any of these terms are used. Except for review purposes, the reproduction of this book in whole or part, electronically or mechanically, constitutes a copyright violation.

For Maya and Padme

Chapter One

Sara lay under the tree on the hill, her back to the horse riding ring, and scratched the dog under its jaw. Waiting for her brother, Josh, to finish his lesson bored her, but she took comfort in petting and snuggling with Ben, the big black Labrador retriever. The lazy, drooling, affectionate dog made the hour at Round Hill Farm tolerable. Sweet Ben had a shiny coat and an old gray face and was gentle, though sometimes he tired of her constant affections and waddled off to find another place to lie down. Today he was patient with her, as she scratched behind his ear and on the dome of his head. He closed his eyes and dropped his head to sleep.

She let him sleep, her fingers moving subconsciously over Ben's scalp as she thought about her life. Josh was still a beginner, and if he kept at this Western riding thing and moved on to rodeo, she would end up spending half her weekends here. Ben the dog represented the only thing she liked about the place. She'd tried riding a horse weeks ago, but found it uninspiring and uncomfortable. She didn't like how much of riding depended on the animal's movements. She wanted to be the one to provide the athletic impetus. *Like when I'd been a gymnast...* She frowned, her eyes still set on the sleeping dog as her thoughts went back in time. *A good gymnast.* *No. I can't think about that. Not now.* But how could she forget when she could still feel the sting in her neck, the old dull ache of her collar bone from where she'd broken it crashing into the mats. *That's behind me. It has to be.*

She returned to her present, boring circumstances. Ben slept; snoring. Lying on her side, Sara craned her neck to check the ring. Josh continued to trot around the ring, looking goofy as he bounced on the bay horse, while the Douglas's daughter, Sharon, called out instructions.

Sara was glad her brother had found something he liked to do. But in a sad sort of way, it made her jealous. She'd been forced to stop doing what she loved.

Gymnastics.

She shifted her thoughts and glanced around back to the dog, then toward a sudden movement downhill.

Near the stable doors, Sara saw a small animal scamper toward the barn: a cat.

She sat up and stared at it. She'd spent countless hours with the cats at Round Hill Farm and knew them all. This one was new. It had a fluffy black and orange tail that shot straight up into the air and some coloring on its haunches and head, the rest of it was white. It was a calico by the looks of it, but a very unusual kind. Rising to her feet, Sara bid Ben goodbye and strode down the hill after the newcomer. She had nothing better to do.

Sixth grade was a drag, most of the kids were snobs and jerks. The lifeless teachers only reached out to the popular kids... kids like Lauren Brimes with her perfect long blonde hair and light blue eyes. Her sickeningly sweet voice, perfect height, and expensive clothes had all of the other students, even seventh and eighth graders, adoring Lauren. *I've got no one and nothing, in school or out.*

The cat disappeared into the barn and Sara followed it. The barn was lit but shadowy. She looked around.

"Where did you go, you rascal?" she said, suddenly feeling silly. *Is this what I've been reduced to — an eleven-year-old girl so lonely, so bored, she has to follow animals around for their affection?*

She checked all the usual places where the barn cats hid: the rafters above the entrances, above the stalls, in the tack room. Finding these spots vacant, she stepped inside the office and saw Munkendoodle, the barn's big tom cat, sitting on the desk as if he owned it. She waved to him and looked around. Flies were everywhere, even in the stable's office. She swatted at a few then turned and crossed the aisle.

Inside the storage alcove sat a covered plastic garbage bin filled with grain. A bucket of tools, brooms, and a shovel leaned against the shadowy timber wall. On the staircase leading to the hayloft sat a cat, but not the new cat with the fluffy tail.

"Hello, Ariel," Sara said. "You catch any rats today?"

The tiny cat with black and white tuxedo markings blinked and rolled over on the narrow plank, nearly losing its balance and tumbling down the steps. When the cat righted itself and stood to arch its back, Sara moved in and stroked it from head to tail.

"You better not have fleas," she said. "Say, have you seen a white cat with a puffy black and orange ringed tail around here somewhere? I'd like to introduce myself."

The tuxedo cat Ariel nudged Sara's hand, showing its teeth while purring.

She gave the cat one good last stroke and then turned to check the stalls.

With my luck the mysterious new cat probably climbed the ladder to the loft.

The thought of going up there after it sent an icy shiver up her spine and to her throat where the impulse choked her. There'd be spiders up there, possibly poisonous black widows. And to get up there, into the hayloft's itchy darkness, she would have to climb a ladder... She would check the stalls first, the empty ones.

Passing the stallion on the left and the Appaloosa on the right, Sara opened the latch to the first vacant stall. Although no horse was kept inside, shavings carpeted the dirt floor. Across from her, the top edge of a kick board had been striped with scratch marks. On a hunch she crept toward the board that reinforced the stable's outer wall against a horse's powerful kick. She stepped on the base beam, grasped the top of the kick board and stood on her toes.

The gap between the stable's outer wall and the kick board was about a foot wide. She peered down into the darkness between and immediately saw glowing yellow eyes staring back up at her.

"Oh, hello?" Sara said. "Are you the cat with the beautiful tail?"

As she scanned the shadows for the feathery, fluffy tail she'd seen earlier, Sara noticed movement from the corner of the narrow space. She gazed at the spot where shavings covered a tangled furry huddle. The light was dim so she slid her arms up on the top of the kick board and dipped her head down into the crevice for a closer look.

The mother cat snarled and hissed so Sara moved her face out of striking range, but the cat did not spring up at her. She gazed back down into the cat's hiding place again and this time was greeted by a soft mewing sound. Staring at the mass of fur and shavings again, she saw a little paw poke out into the light, then a tiny ear, and finally she saw a tiny pair of glowing yellow eyes. A kitten!

As the pile came apart, she noticed a second pair of eyes, sleepy and half-closed but with enough shininess to pierce up through the dark crevice. Not one kitten but—Sara counted what she believed to be individual kittens—two, three, and four. Four kittens!

Like their mother, they were all mostly white. One had a black forehead and black tail, and another had a gray head and tail, while a third had a few orange patches here and there amid its otherwise vanilla coat. All of the newborns had fluffy tails but the fourth had the fluffiest of all, even rivaling the mother's. Sara stared in wonder. The mother cat stared back as one of the kittens mewed, then another, and Sara realized she should probably leave the cat family alone. The kittens were likely hungry and their mother wouldn't let them nurse with a stupid human peering down at them.

She jumped back down and trotted out of the stall, running through the aisle and out of the barn. *The Douglases should know about this,* she told herself. *Cats choose the craziest places to have kittens,* she thought as she ran toward the house.

Chapter Two

The owners of the farm, Fred and Phyllis Douglas, were an elderly, retired couple, and in her excitement it was hard for Sara to wait for them to amble after her as she led the way to the barn.

"You didn't know there were kittens in there?" Sara asked, glancing back as she neared the stable doors.

Huffing, Mrs. Douglas said, "No, like I said we have stray cats coming in all the time. All the cats just wandered here at some point or another. People drop them off near farmhouses thinking we'll take them in to help us keep the rodent population down."

Sara nodded and stood outside the empty stall. "In here," she said waving them over.

Fred Douglas arrived and unlatched the door. He held it open for Mrs. Douglas, who went inside. Sara followed and pointed. "Over there, near the corner. Look down behind that board."

Phyllis Douglas stepped onto the support beam and looked down into the crevice. She was tall enough that she didn't need to stand on her toes as Sara had done. "My goodness," the woman said. "How precious."

Her husband came over for a look, standing to the left of Mrs. Douglas. "Well, look at that," he said. "More kittens. Just what we need," he added sarcastically.

"Now, Fred, I think it's beautiful," Mrs. Douglas said, still staring down at the mewing kittens and their protective mother. "And besides, when's the last time you saw a rat trying to get into the grain bin? Around a barn, cats are a good thing."

"I know," Fred said, shaking his head, "but they eat all the poor birds and rabbits, too...even though I pay a fortune on cat food." He shook his head again. "We have too many cats around here already."

Mrs. Douglas turned to Sara, who'd been waiting for another look at the kittens. "Do you have a cat, Sara?" she said with a mischievous smile.

Oh, no. Not that. I can barely take care of myself.
"No," she replied at last. "We have a dog. A collie. Why?"

Mrs. Douglas grinned. "How would you like a kitten?" She motioned with her head toward the wall of the stall. "I'll give you pick of the litter."

Sara stammered. "I–I couldn't. I..."

"Now, Sara, I know you're good with animals. Ol' Ben hasn't had so much attention since he was a puppy. Why don't you ask your mom if you can take one home?"

As Sara thought about it a sudden flush of warmth rose in her chest and cut through any further hesitation. She stepped on the beam and gazed down into the poorly lit cat nursery, enjoying all of the kittens, but looking for the one she'd noticed earlier. It had been the smallest, the most albino, and by the way it staggered when it moved, the weakest. The one with the funniest and fluffiest tail in the litter.

"Fred," Mrs. Douglas said, "why don't you go grab a flashlight, so Sara can get a better look at them?"

Mr. Douglas returned from the tack room with a big yellow flashlight and pointed it down between the boards. The mother cat blinked and hissed at the light intruding on her kittens.

Sara checked over the litter and focused on her favorite. The fluffy kitten with tiny dark brown and orange colored triangles on its head. Compared with the rest of the litter, the kitten's almost entirely white coat had the least number of colored splotches on it. Only its head, one tiny paw, hindquarters, and tail had any coloring: brown and orange. The kitten's half-closed eyes were yellow, and from its overall demeanor it looked needy and confused, but not frightened. "*Mew*," the kitten called upon its mother before any further cries were quickly drowned out by its siblings.

Her eyes never leaving it, Sara said, "I like the shy one there."

She pointed. The flashlight highlighted the kitten's fluffy, multicolored tail wrapped around its hind quarters.

"Would you look at that plume," Mrs. Douglas said.

"Yeah, I'll take that one," Sara said with a giggle.

Chapter Three

Rustic and sunlit, the palace on the Turkish lake was old, centuries old, and the villagers from the neighboring town often glanced from their chores in the foothills for a glimpse of the charming ruins gracing the valley. It was beautiful but frightening to the women and children who gathered grapes on the hillside. Too often in the midday sun, it seemed their eyes played tricks on them.

The quiet murmurs among the villagers were of a surviving member of the once-royal family still living within the crumbling walls of the ancient fortress. Though this was only a rumor, the regional chief had forbidden any of them to trespass on the Orkhan property. The chief had even turned away a visiting professor of antiquities in 2015, so that the Lake Van region could continue to respectfully ignore the once-royal palace grounds, which, despite reports of a sole owner and occupant, continued to fall into decay. Little was known about the family's final descendant. Some said he was mad, delusional, still believing his bloodline was that of the true Sultan ruling class.

Inside the palace's darkest and only windowless room, a man stood on his head and stared into the eyes of a furry cat. His long, thin, black hair spilled over the silk covered pillow, the weight of his body forcing a reversal of blood and spirit. His palms and the tips of his fingers pressed firmly into the soft carpet on either side of the pillow. He straightened his legs above, the heels of his bare feet resting against the tiled wall. More blood rushed to his head as he stared into the feline's glimmering yellow eyes. Surrounding the cat's dark pupils, the yellow-green pigment bore the imperfections of some precious gem, an intricate iris in which he could get lost if he did not remain in control.

Control was mandatory, and fortunately for him his own eyes could be just as hypnotic as the cat's—he possessed penetrating dark brown eyes that, with a sustained gaze, could take control of whatever they wished. From the stuffed cat he stole answers. He'd posed the cat so close that his proudly inverted hawk nose inhaled just a whisker from the cat's far-flatter, pink nose. Despite the intensity of his stare, the man's breathing was slow, in relaxed meditation.

The cat, on the other hand, while possessing many answers did not breathe. It hadn't breathed for centuries, since the reign of the first Orkhan, the first true Sultan, who upon the prized feline's death had ordered the animal stuffed and mounted in a standing position, its fluffy plume-like tail held high. Mostly white with mid-length fur, the cat had an orange and brown-ringed tail and several small triangular markings of the same colors on its head. White tufts curled from its lifeless paws, as if to hint at the curved claws retracted inside the feline's toes.

The man had scrutinized the mounted cat for many years since he'd inherited it from his father, who long before inherited it from his own father. He'd studied it from the points of its furry ears to the tapered tip of its bushy tail. Today, however, he fixed his gaze on the cat's glassy eyes and the visions they induced. From the headstand, the increased blood flow to his brain allowed him to better sense things. Like the misshapen mole on his forehead, which now itched at such an inopportune time. If he reached up to scratch it, he would have to go one-handed, and this exercise was about concentration. So he ignored this regular irritation and in a perfectly relaxed state he attempted to steal knowledge from the stuffed cat.

It was written in divination, or fortune-telling, a diviner must straddle the line between pushing and pulling, giving and taking, projecting his thoughts and listening. The last Orkhan realized if he allowed the cat's eyes to take control, the animal would transport him to a time and place unrelated to the treasure he sought.

Through a twinkle in the cat's green-gold iris, an image of his great-great-grandfather materialized in Orkhan's mind's eye. He recognized his ancestor from the painted portrait he'd seen many times in the palace's gallery, whose walls, on the other side of the palace, had recently collapsed. In the vision his great-great-grandfather limped and his face suffered the gauntness of age. He carried a crate, an elaborate container for his prized cat, a cat similar to the stiff one whose eyes Orkhan gazed into in the present.

Vague information flooded Orkhan Hamid's brain. He wore a contented grin as he continued to meditate. The image of his great-great-grandfather under a tent with his cat, showing off a breed the American men and women around him had never before seen or heard of.

In a surprise burst, the cat ran away, and Great-Great-Grandfather growled and sobbed in agony. Orkhan felt a sudden sympathetic pang for his ancestor's futility at trying to recover the cat and at his great loss of spirit and soul. In the vision, the old man's eyes lost their hope, his arthritis grew worse as the last of the empire turned to a republic in the country of Turkey, and the title of Sultan, whether recognized or not, was to be no more. His great-great-grandfather died at the age of eighty-one.

The cat! I must have the cat! So where did you go, oh, turner of fortune?

His grandfather told him the stories as a boy. The last of any dignity the family possessed scampered away from them that day in Virginia, where Great-Great-Grandfather's, the first Orkhan Hamid's, wealthy American supporters had hosted him. Such a great loss. A great, heart-breaking, soul-sucking loss. The histories and destinies of this breed of lake cat and the true Sultan Orkhan family had been intertwined since the time of the flood. Grandpa had shown him the illustrations from one of the family's many sacred books. The original settlements by the lake, gorgeous illustrations of the village men and their cats swimming together in the lake...books now rotting inside the toppled shelves of the library...

I must have that cat.
But where?
Once again he focused his sharp eyes on America, using the stuffed cat as his conduit.
I need good fortune.
I want that cat and will do anything to get it!
His eyes focused, then rolled up behind his brow. He envisioned a forest, the cat creeping through it, both a predator and, due to its modest size, as potential prey.

The cat journeyed through the forest in Orkhan's mind, the feline sticking to cover, creeping through the brush, staying behind trees, stones, and human structures. In a lake by a fishing shack, it dove into a pond and returned to shore with a sunfish in its mouth. Another flash across Orkhan's brain. The cat wandered more, encountering peasant American cats, worthless strays. *Blast you if you've weakened the purity of my cat!*

He relaxed when in the next vision, the cat returned in its still pure form. But this time as a kitten. His body quivered as the realization hit him: One has survived.

The mother had taken shelter in a horse barn to have her litter. One of the kittens appeared to have all marks of the noblest Turkish Van blood. Plume-like tail, tufts of fur from its toes and ears, and a love of water. The bloodline remained strong right up to the present day...

He saw an elderly couple intruding behind the wall of the stall where the litter blinked up at them, four kittens with shavings caught in their fur. Orkhan saw a girl with dark curls and dark skin staring down at the kittens, her timid yet hopeful eyes locking onto his cat. He took mental pictures of this girl, and beckoned the stuffed cat for one more answer.

"It is my cat," Orkhan muttered. "Return to me what rightfully belongs to me, Almighty."

The vision started to blur, the image of the fluffy chosen one disappeared—but in its wake the stuffed cat's yellow eyes glowed, and Orkhan was granted the image of a white wooden sign. Nailed crookedly to the rural highway fence, the lettered panel revealed a clue to the location. Sloppy block strokes of black paint said: Westmoreland.

"I've found you," Orkhan croaked as a tear rolled down his cheek.

"At last, I've found you."

Chapter Four

For the entire car ride home, Sara thought about the kitten she had chosen. Finally, something of her very own she could share secrets with, to cuddle when she needed comfort, or just to play with to get her mind off her chronic pain reminding her constantly of everything she'd lost.

"If you want a kitten, you are going to be the one who takes care of it," Mom said, interrupting Sara's thoughts. She emphasized the word *you*.

"I will, Mom."

Without turning from the wheel, Mrs. Danielle Massey said, "Which means feeding and brushing it daily. But most importantly…cleaning the litter box."

"Not a problem, Mom," Sara said, swallowing. "I'll do it."

"You better," Mom said. "Lincoln is enough work as it is."

Lincoln was the family dog, an easy-going five-year-old collie which hadn't been any trouble since he'd had a few accidents on the carpet as a puppy. Sara wondered how the dog and new kitten would get along when they finally met. The plan was to let the kitten nurse from its mother at the barn for another month before bringing it home to Percyville.

She couldn't wait.

🐈

When Monday came, Sara's sixth-grade classes passed painfully slow. She thought about her kitty the entire time. Until that kitty with the fluffy raccoon-like tail was hers, there was no use in trying to focus on her schoolwork. She had to have it now or she was certain she'd flunk out for sure.

During her free period before lunch, Sara walked to the library. Peering in through the glass walls she saw the library was empty. Except for Miss Walters the librarian, which was why Sara had come here often since sixth grade had started two weeks ago. The library gave her a chance to get away from the groups of sixth and seventh graders who all hung out together and gave her the cold shoulder or, in Lauren Brimes's case, angry glares and insulting remarks about her clothes and where they'd been purchased.

She went inside and walked the aisle between the reception area and shelves to the computer desk against the far wall. Sitting down, she typed into the search bar the word "calico."

The results appeared and she clicked on the first one but didn't find it helpful so she tried a few more linked articles and once again came up empty. She added the word "cat" to the bar and hit the search button.

Now this is more like it. Inside the top right window of the computer screen, she saw several thumbnail-sized photos of the multicolored cats. They were black, white, and orange-bodied, their markings coming in a variety of patterns that seemed to have little pattern at all. None of the cats pictured so far had fluffy tails. She opened one of the featured articles and read.

The cat's predominant colors, the article said, were white, orange tabby, and black. *All check so far,* she mused. The article also said calico was not technically a breed, and a number of different breeds could be considered calico with their color patterns, including something called the Japanese bobtail. Most calico cats were females. *Hmm, I didn't know that.* She clicked on the link for the Japanese bobtail and saw that this breed of cat had very little tail at all. *Just like its name*, she thought, remembering bobcats had stubby little tails. *This is silly. I'm never going to find what breed my new kitty is—*

"What are you doing, weirdo?" a sneering voice interrupted Sara's thoughts.

Sara spun around in the chair and saw Lauren Brimes, her arms crossed, face twisted in contempt. With her were Donna Sutherland and Zoe Fallon, Lauren's two best friends, who liked to join Lauren in everything including teasing unpopular students. *Unpopular like me,* Sara moaned to herself. The three girls wore pretty dresses you'd see in the pages of a fashion magazine. Beautiful, soft hair with stylish, silk scarves wrapped around their necks. Of course their pierced ears with shiny earrings, expensive shoes, and perfect complexions topped off the model like package Sara could never compete with. Which of course also meant she'd never have a chance at belonging in the elite inner circle of the 'cool girls.' Which Lauren and her cronies often took delight in reminding Sara of with their off-the-cuff, snide, snobby little digs.

"I said, what are you doing?" Lauren repeated. She peered over Sara's shoulder. "Looking at cat photos? How stupid," she said with a scoff.

Sara's eyes moved from Lauren to Donna to Zoe, then back to Lauren. Deciding it best to remain calm she said, "Yeah, I'm getting a cat from the barn where my brother rides, and I wanted to find out what breed she is. She has this unique tail and strange markings on her head and I'm going to write my English paper about how special—"

"You're not getting a special cat, you idiot," Lauren said mockingly and on cue Donna and Zoe snickered. "Your cat is a barn cat, a stray. And it's probably deformed..." Lauren paused. "...just like you."

Sara winced. That hurt. And once again Donna and Zoe laughed, loudly this time until Miss Walters got up to shush them. The librarian put her hands on her hips and glared at Lauren, the school's most social sixth-grader, and an enemy to a quiet library.

"Let's go, girls," Lauren said and the trio strode out in formation with Lauren leading the way, leaving Sara shaken and holding her chest.

Struggling not to cry, Sara shut off the Internet browser, removing the images that had briefly made her so curious and happy.

Why are they so mean to me? she pondered with an aching in her chest. *What did I ever do to them? Is there something wrong with me that makes them single me out like this?*

Alone in the library, she slouched in the chair.

It hadn't been the first time Sara had been targeted. Last week, Lauren made fun of her hair in front of the entire lunch table stating how it was all kinky and greasy. To fit in here, to be liked, she needed straight hair like Lauren and most of the other girls and boys. She wanted to go back to North Carolina where she had friends more like her.

Grabbing her books, Sara reluctantly got up from the desk. *Time for history class.* Lauren, Donna, and Zoe would be in the class with her.

Not looking forward to this. Sara trudged out of the library, dread building in her gut with every step.

Chapter Five

She sat with a skinny little blond boy on the bus ride home. Like her, this boy wasn't welcome to sit with any of the other student passengers and had to wander awkwardly up and down the aisle of the bus trying to find a seat where someone might accept him. He plopped down next to Sara and released a small sigh.

His name was Jimmy Schneider, and Sara remembered how on the first day of school he'd slid into an empty seat unaware of the reason why some of the seventh grade boys had been standing or leaning over the seat backs to watch him. The sudden wetness on the bottom of his trousers had caused him to stand up and turn to check his bottom while many of the other students had laughed. They had spat all over the vinyl-covered seat and left the seat empty for the first unsuspecting student. Poor Jimmy had been that unsuspecting and unfortunate student, his pants sopping wet from the puddle of spit. He'd cried and thrown up the rest of the bus ride home, with the driver having to pull the bus over to get Jimmy a bag. Sara hadn't known they'd set a trap for him until it was too late and felt great pity for him ever since. She liked whenever he sat with her. She knew how he felt—sort of. At least today Jimmy's trousers weren't soaked with spit. She cleared her throat. "How were classes today?"

Without looking up from his lap where his backpack rested, Jimmy issued a shy reply, "Okay."

She stared at him, hoping he'd make eye contact, but he didn't. "Same here," she said and then looked straight ahead for the rest of the ride. The bus would stop and students would get off, and the bus would start off again. All of the other kids talked, but no one spoke a word to her or Jimmy.

Mercifully her stop on North Canal Street came and the bus stopped. She walked down the aisle, facing forward, ignoring the sneaky glances or contemptuous glares from the other students. Her backpack slung over her shoulder, she stepped down to the sidewalk and plodded toward her house, head down.

She let herself in and locked the door behind her. Her brother would be home in about an hour after his drama class and her mother in time to make dinner. In the meantime, she was forbidden to go outside or let anyone inside. Not that she had any friends knocking the door down to spend time with her.

Alone again, she thought... Except for Lincoln, who stared sadly at her from beside his food bowl, hoping for an early supper. He was a full-size collie, with a long coat everywhere except his face and legs. His coat was a light golden tan with black highlights, his chest and paws were white. She stared back into his expectant eyes and from his sitting position he shifted impatiently, licking his chops.

"No, Linky," she said in the same affectionate voice she always used with the dog. "It's not time for your din-din yet." She patted him on the head and continued past him into the hall toward her bedroom.

Tossing her book bag on the floor, she turned on the radio and collapsed on her bed. As much as she loved that beggar dog out there, and as much as he depended on her, she still felt terribly alone. Percyville wasn't anything like Charlotte, North Carolina, where she at least had a few friends. Here it was starting over and no one was giving her a chance.

With a sniffle, Sara wiped the back of her hand over her face and stopped herself from crying. On the radio a song was playing by the new teen star, Beverly Diaz, and although she liked the song, she didn't feel like hearing it right now. It was a sad song about a girl who'd lost her boyfriend to another girl, and the fact that Sara didn't know any boys made the song that much more pathetically tear-jerking. She rolled off the bed to her feet and returned to the kitchen. Maybe she would feed Lincoln and then let him out, and afterwards see if he might come up on her bed and let her hug him.

Her mother's "when-at-home-alone" instructions also included her doing her homework, but Sara didn't have the will for that now. Drearily, she served Lincoln his kibble, and when he was done scarfing it up she called him over to the back door, unlocked it and sent him out to the penned-in area where he went to the bathroom.

She leaned against the wall, slowly sliding into a slumping seated position on the floor of the back hall.

Moving her legs into butterfly position, she stretched. A sharp bark beckoned her minutes later, and she let Lincoln back in and locked up again. She had a biscuit ready for him and teased him with it, all the way to her bed. "Come on up, Linky! Jump!"

The collie leapt on the bed, devoured the bone-shaped treat, and then circled the mattress, sniffing. She patted the mattress next to her. "Here, boy. Lie down, boy."

Lincoln stared at her and whimpered.

"What's the matter, boy?"

He stepped toward the edge of the bed and jumped down, gazing back almost apologetically before disappearing down the hall.

Doesn't anyone want to be with me? Glumly, Sara retrieved her book bag, brought it to her desk and worked on her math homework until she heard the sound of her brother's car in the driveway. Placing her pencil down, she returned to the kitchen and waited for Josh at the door.

Her brother was a slender, six-foot-tall sixteen-year-old, more bone than brawn, with curly brown hair sticking up everywhere and dangling down to his shoulders. He'd gotten his driver's license in August, just in time for the school year and despite his awkwardness, he was having an easier time of it than her. After switching his focus from beginner rodeo to drama class, Josh had made a lot of new high school friends, boys and girls alike, with whom he went out for movies, burgers and shakes, and ice cream sundaes.

As a result of visiting the Douglas's farm a lot less, she no longer got to see the fluffy-tailed kitten to whom she would be engaged. She was happy for her brother, although a bit envious she had not found something she loved to do in which she, too, could make friends.

"How was drama practice?" she asked.

Josh forked his fingers through his curls. "Okay, thanks... Uh, did you feed Link?"

"You ask me every day. Yeah."

"Let him out?"

"He's supposed to be your dog. But yeah, I let him out."

He gave her a half-hearted smile. "Good. I have tons of homework. I'll be in my room." He carried his backpack to his room, and Lincoln trotted after him. Sara heard the door close behind him.

"Great, just great," she said to no one. "Even my own brother doesn't give me the time of day." Returning to her room, she slammed the door shut and sat down at her desk and continued her homework.

But she wasn't able to focus. Inside the unwelcoming walls of junior high school and even in their neighborhood, her lack of friends left her with nothing. What made it worse was dad's leaving following the divorce, and her abrupt end to gymnastics.

The homework, trying to determine the difference between the associative, communicative, distributive, and multiplicative properties of this and that, was just another missing piece of the puzzle that was her unhappy life. She dropped her pencil, and lowered her head into her hands as a splitting headache added to her misery.

Chapter Six

Weeks passed, the same routine plaguing her: no friends, D's on her math quizzes, C's on science and history tests, and a B on her uninspired English paper about the only excitement in her life, the upcoming arrival of her cat. Even Physical Education class became a source of dread as her gymnastics injury from two years ago made her timid toward physical activity. Phys Ed also meant locker room time with the other girls, including the abusive Lauren Brimes and her inseparable book-ends, Donna and Zoe. Last week, they'd grabbed her shorts before she could put them on and thrown them on top of the lockers, making her late for class in the gym. After Sara found the custodian, Mr. Ambrose, and gotten him to retrieve her shorts, she'd run into the gym and Miss Munchak greeted her with the shrillness of her whistle, as she did to all tardy students. Sara could hear Lauren and some of the others chuckling but Sara Massey was not a snitch. She didn't know the school well enough and what might happen if she whined to Miss Munchak about why she'd been late.

Weekends offered little comfort from the cruel school time. She'd either accompany her mom grocery shopping, listen to music in her room, or draw pictures of cats and dogs that she knew weren't any good. Only trips to Round Hill Farm, which gave her a chance to peek down behind the kick board at the fluffy-tailed mother cat and her kittens, gave her happiness.

On the third week of her wait to have the kitten, while her busy brother rode inside the ring, she went into the stable and looked down at the mostly white kitty with the black and orange triangles on top of its head and the fluffy tail.

"You sure you want to come home with a loser like me?"

The kitten staggered around, shavings in its fur, exploring the small space, its eyes open more than the last time she'd seen it. But it did not answer.

Sara sighed. "I hope so. Because you're the only bright spot in my life right now, little cutie."

And finally the day to pick up the kitten came. Sara's mom drove them to the pet supply store for a kitty carrier, a carton of litter, cat food, and some toys.

The weather was pleasant as they headed toward the stable, a cloudless sky and the sun was hot and bright as they parked and walked toward the barn, her mom carrying the kitty carrier. Sara glanced around. There were many young cats running around, but none of them were her fluffy-tailed kitten or its mother.

Inside the horse stable, more of the wild cats scattered, all of them ordinary looking. "Let's check the wall," Sara said.

Opening the stall, they checked and to Sara's dismay there wasn't a single feline in the snug spot where her kitty had been born. "I hope she didn't run away," she said.

If my only hope, the kitten, has run away...then so will I, she decided.

"Let's keep looking," Mom said, distracting Sara from her self-pity.

Sara spotted a cat with a bushy tail near the grain bin: it was the mother cat.

"Hey there, beautiful," she said. "Where's your pretty little daughter with the raccoon tail?"

The cat meowed and rubbed the grain canister but when Sara went to pet her, the cat trotted off. Sara and her mother turned back toward the stalls, and that's when they saw the kitten.

"Is that the one?" Mom asked.

Sara tiptoed toward the kitten, its mother far enough away so if she grabbed it, mama cat would have to cover several yards to strike at her. "Yes," she whispered, answering her own mother. She stole closer.

Mom snorted. "Look at that tail," she said. "It's like the plume on a French hat."

Sara reached for the kitten but not quickly enough, and it mewed and scurried away. The mother cat whirled and stared at Sara.

"Darn! Mom, help me corner her."

"I have an idea," Sara's mother said, and then she disappeared through the rear doors of the stable.

Sara carefully passed the mother cat and followed the kitten as it walked crookedly toward the front door, its plume-like tail raised high.

To Sara's delight, her mother appeared outside the stable's front entrance, blocking the kitten's escape and the little kitty spun and with a squeak angled toward the empty stable where it had been born.

The brown horse in the closest stall lowered its head and the kitten, suddenly spooked, leapt up and swatted at the horse's nose. The horse jerked its head up in time, the kitty's paw missing by a whisker, and in the confusion the kitten changed course, scampered past Sara, and then ducked into the shadowy storage area.

"Oh, you missed your chance!" Mom cried.

Though disappointed she hadn't grabbed the kitten, Sara couldn't help but laugh. The kitty had taken a swipe at a horse, an animal hundreds of times its own size and weight. *What a little showoff. This cat thinks it's the boss,* she thought.

"She's a vicious little kitten, Mom," she said. "I think we'd better take it slow with this one. Hey kitty, come here." She made a clicking sound with her tongue.

In the corner of the stable, partially hidden behind a yellow antifreeze container, the kitten sat still and looked at her with a "you've-got-to-be-kidding-me" expression.

"Come on, show me that pretty tail of yours again," Sara said. "Come here."

"*Rrrr-inttt,*" the kitten mewed, and scuttled over to Sara's hand, possibly thinking she had food of some sort. It sniffed, showing its teeth, and then spun, the plume-like tail raised high in the air. The kitten rubbed against Sara's leg, its fluffy, feathery, multicolored tail tickling her behind the knee.

Sara giggled. "I'm glad she likes me, Mom."
Then the kitten wheeled and leapt, landing on Sara's arm before she could react. Tiny claws dug into Sara's skin, then the kitten cocked its head and bit.

"Ow!" Sara shook her arm.

The kitten leapt down and scooted away, making its *rrrr-intt* sound as it ran.

To her mother, Sara said, "Her claws are just ticklish at this point but her teeth are sharp. And she's pretty quick and good at hiding. I guess getting her into the kitty carrier is going to be hard."

"Like herding cats," her mother said.

"What?"

"Oh, never mind." Mom started after the escaped kitten. "Help me corner her and put her in this thing. You would think Mr. and Mrs. Douglas would have had her ready for us."

"I told you already, Mom. They tried. The kitty's too wild and fast for them. They'd prefer we do it."

"Good luck to us, then," Mom said.

"Well, at least its mother isn't overprotecting it any more. You should have seen the first time I tried to touch one of those kittens."

"Right." Mom headed toward the doors. "I'll go around the outside again and come in through the front door."

When Sara and her mother converged again, their heads nearly collided as the kitten with the fluffy tail evaded their grasp and disappeared inside the empty stall. They followed it in and Sara's mom shut the creaking door behind her. In the shadowy corner, the kitten was struggling to climb the kick board to its place of birth. It was halfway up the wall before Sara reached for it.

Like a fly with eyes in the back of its head, the kitten saw her coming and jumped down and ran right at Mom, who was blocking the already shut door. The woman shrieked as the fast little cat leapt at her, clawing and climbing her knee, her chest, and finally her shoulder. Using the woman's shoulder as a launching platform, the kitten sprang for the barred open portion of the stall door. It fell short, but managed to cling to the wood panel and climb. It was nearly to the bars, meant to keep a horse from trying to jump out. But for a cat the opening between those bars meant escape!

"Quick, Mom!" Sara cried.

Mom seized the kitten and carried it from the opening. She bent down and put it in the crate, Sara rushed over to shut and latch the door before the wild kitten could escape.

Chapter Seven

The unveiling of Sara's new kitten occurred in the kitchen, with Josh on hand now to witness what all the fuss had been about. The kitty mewed the entire ride home, probably wondering why it had been snatched from its mommy, brother and sisters, and fellow barn cats. Mom had arranged long in advance for vaccinations at the veterinary hospital, and before coming home the vet had given the kitty all the necessary vaccinations to prevent things like rabies and tetanus.

The long trip to the barn and the vet had been both exhausting and painful, the car ride causing Sara's body to stiffen and her neck to throb. It was the old fracture from her gymnastics injury again. But the anticipation of introducing the kitten to her new home had kept Sara going. Wincing, she knelt and unlatched the crate, then made a clucking sound to call the kitty out of hiding. When the kitten didn't come out, Sara lowered her head and peered inside the crate.

"Now, Sara, be careful that she doesn't scratch your eyes out."

Ignoring her mother, Sara stared at the kitten. It looked frightened and a bit dazed. "Don't be scared little kitty. I won't hurt you."

The kitten stared back at her and mewed sadly.

Sara reached into the crate.

"Sara, don't!"

She pulled the kitten out and stood up, holding it in her arms, its head against her heart, one hand scooped under its lower spine, the other cradling its shoulders. "It's not a mean kitty, Mom. It's...I mean, she's...a little angel." She stroked the cat's scalp with her fingernails.

Finally, Josh said something in his usual dry tone. "Gee, what a strange looking thing. Its tail is outrageous."

"It's not a tail, doofus," Sara scolded. "It's a plume, and she's not an 'it,' she's a she."

Then Lincoln trotted in, wondering what all the commotion was about and the kitten hissed and twisted in Sara's arms, scratching her wrist. Sara let go and the kitten landed on its feet and took off after the dog. The collie froze in fear as the strange newcomer came up to him brazenly, stood on her hind paws, and batted the dog's snout.

"Don't hit my dog!" Josh picked up the kitten and placed it down beside Sara. "Come on, Link. Let's go watch Glee reruns."

Sara watched her brother lead the uninjured but shaken collie into the family den.

"Did she get you?" Mom asked.

Sara checked her wrist. The kitten had left a pair of two-inch scrapes, barely piercing the skin. "Not too bad," she said. Her eyes landed on the kitty, which had started to explore the kitchen, her long bushy tail dragging along the linoleum floor. It really was a plume.

"I think I'll call her Plume." She watched Plume sniff the leg of one of the kitchen stools. "What do you think, Mom?"

Mom moved to see where the kitten was going. Plume had found the dog's water bowl and stopped to drink, lapping the liquid up with her tiny, pale-pink tongue.

Mom laughed. "You better fill her her own water bowl, Sara. She's a thirsty little girl."

The neck pain subsided, and for the first time in a long time, Sara felt pure joy tingling through her from head to toe. She had a new friend: a wild and furry little friend that had what could possibly be the world's fluffiest tail. *Plume.*

Plume liked to jump up on things, and Sara and her mom quickly learned how hard it was to keep the active kitten off the furniture and out of trouble. They'd gotten her two scratching posts, one that was like a tree house, but Plume ignored all these attempts to quell her wild streak and dug her claws into the side of the sofa and the dog often.

At one-point Mom had yelled, "Get your claws out of my sofa or I'll have you declawed, you feral fiend!"

"Mom!" Sara had scolded. "Declawing is cruel!"

"I know. I was only kidding, honey. But we can't afford a new sofa if she wrecks that one."

Plume also liked anything associated with water. Her fascination included sinks, bathtubs and toilets, which when not closely guarded she scaled and investigated. One day when Josh had left the toilet lid open, despite constant reminders to shut it, Plume had jumped up on the rim. When Sara had entered for her turn in the bathroom she'd seen the cat slip and fall into the toilet. The kitten quickly recovered, scrambling out of the basin and then bursting out of the bathroom, going right between Sara's legs while she stood in the doorway.

When Sara told her mother and Josh why Plume's paws and fluffy tail were wet, they'd all laughed for a long time and made jokes until Sara's mom said, "I wonder what this fascination with water is all about. Don't cats normally hate water?"

It was true. They'd all used a spray bottle to try to train Plume from jumping on the dinner table and kitchen counter, where, for instance, she'd helped herself to a few mouthfuls of Mom's casserole. But Plume had not minded the hard spray of water and had kept doing whatever naughty thing she'd been doing.

Often, after brushing her teeth, Sara would return to the bathroom to find Plume in the sink, licking the water leaking from the faucet. There was something oddly different about this cat, and Sara wanted to know what that thing was. Part of her told her, in the dull sadness of her life, her imagination was getting the best of her, causing her to want to be associated with something special. Not some ordinary barn cat as the cruel, heartless Lauren Brimes had teased. Not some ordinary calico. Plume was different in so many odd ways. She didn't act like an ordinary cat.

Chapter Eight

The plumber came one hectic Wednesday morning to fix the faulty bathtub drain. The clogged drain annoyed Sara, Josh, and Mom for two reasons. First, it took an eternity for the accumulated bath or shower water to drain, which left a scum that was difficult to clean. Second, Plume liked to pounce around and play in the puddle inside the tub at every opportunity. Sara and her mom worried Plume might try to drink the disgusting, scummy water.

The garbage men were outside her bedroom window picking up the trash, the recycling team would be by soon, and Sara was in danger of missing her bus. Hectic wasn't the word for today; today was that other 'H' word. She thought maybe she'd get lucky and the bus would get stuck in traffic and be late today, or maybe Josh would drop her off on his way to the high school. The front door slammed shut...nope, that was him leaving.

Then, from the bathroom down the hall she heard a frightened holler followed by the sound of hearty laughter. She reached the bathroom and peered inside. On the rim of the tub, Plume stood swishing her tail furiously. From what Sara could tell, her baby cat had just been curious, wanting to watch the plumber work.

"What happened?" she said.

The plumber was a plump, gray-haired, good old boy in overalls. He grinned at Sara as he knelt in the tub. "Your cat jumped—" he stopped to chuckle, "—on my back as I leaned down to snake the drain."

Sara laughed. She could picture that. Plume had climbed on her own back a few days ago while she'd been cleaning the litter box. *It must be Plume's curiosity. To watch me and now the plumber work.*

"And then she jumped down and started pawing at the water buildup, you know, kind of splashing me with it. Hilarious."

Sara's mom came up behind her and peered in. "Hi, Jeff," she said. "Need me?"

"Nah," Jeff said. "I was just getting to know your cat. She won't leave me alone," he said with another chuckle.

"It's the water," Sara said. "She's a water cat."

"Here, let me get her," Mom said, slipping past Sara.

"That's okay," the plumber said. "I don't mind. She's kind of cute and so fluffy. I don't think I've ever seen a cat with a tail like that."

Despite Jeff's politeness, Mom lifted Plume, who mewed a protest. "Cat, we need to let Jeff work in peace and fix our drain." She carried the kitten out of the bathroom and Sara followed her.

"Mom, do you think you can give me a ride to school on your way to work? I think I'm gonna miss the bus."

Mom frowned. "I can't leave while the plumber is here, hon. Why don't you just run out now? And if you've missed it, I'll take you in later and explain things."

"But I didn't have time to make my lunch."

"Get hot lunch today."

Sara strode off, shaking her head. Another bus ride with Lauren and her two evil puppets, Donna and Zoe. *Real fun*, she thought letting out a whimper. Something brushed her shin and she looked down. It was Plume and the kitten was looking up as she rubbed against Sara, the kitty's fluffy tail wrapping around Sara's leg, the tip tickling behind her knee. Plume meowed, and Sara reached down to stroke the kitty's back.

"I'll see you after school, beauty," she told her kitty and then ran for the bus, grabbing her book bag on the way.

Following an uneventful bus ride to school, long day of classes, and a loud and smelly bus ride home, Sara returned to a house empty of all but the pets. She knew something was wrong the moment she walked in the door. Lincoln was not in the kitchen, his tail wagging, waiting for her with that feed-me-early look. Sara put her books down and headed for the den where the dog's favorite bed was located against the wall, not far from the fireplace. To her astonishment the bed was occupied, but not by Lincoln.

"Plume, how dare you steal Lincoln's bed," she scolded teasingly.

Plume licked a paw and rubbed it over her ear and brow. While Sara and her family had been gone for the day, Plume had taken over the household, and the kitten, nestled in the center indentation created by Lincoln's many years of use, had even taken over the dog's bed.

"Now I've seen it all," Sara said. "Our dog has surrendered to your supremacy, your highness, Princess Plume." Sara bowed.

Plume's yellow eyes watched her blankly for a moment, then the kitten got up, stretched and walked over to rub Sara's leg. Sara bent down to stroke the kitten's back. "Aww, did you miss me?"

The kitten tilted her head back and made eye contact. She meowed and then rubbed Sara's leg some more, circling her, happy to see her.

Sara picked up her kitten and placed her so Plume was looking back over her shoulder. "Come on, Princess Plume. Let's find that big old dog you scared."

🐈

They found Lincoln in Mom's room, on the bed, the dog's sanctuary whenever he was sick or frightened.

"You two are eventually going to be friends, right?" Sara said, glancing from Plume on her shoulder to the shivering collie on the bed.

Lincoln put his head down timidly. Sara didn't want to force the issue so she carried the kitten to her bedroom. She placed Plume on the bed, which was unmade from when she'd left it in her morning haste, and closed the bedroom door behind her. She went into the bathroom to wash her hands. When she returned the kitten was gone from the spot where she'd left her. Sara sat on the edge of the mattress to take off her shoes and then crawled into bed and pulled the sheet over her head. "Here, kitty kitty," she called sweetly.

Sara waited, listening. She knew her closet door was closed so Plume couldn't have gotten in there. Maybe the kitten was exploring behind her dresser or had gone under the bed. There wasn't any water in the room so what possible trouble could the kitty get in? She would take a quick nap and then feed both pets. *Just a quick little nap and feed them before Josh and Mom get home.* She shut her eyes and relaxed.

Once asleep, she awoke to the sensation of something poking at her stomach. Removing the sheet from her face, she lifted her head and Plume trotted up her chest and pressed her wet pink nose to Sara's nose. Sara giggled, and then for the first time she noticed the rusty partial mustache on the left side of the kitty's snout.

"You have odd markings," she said. Plume turned around and stretched out, her fat, feathery tail covering Sara's chin. She giggled as Plume began kneading her belly with her tiny undeveloped claws. The plume-like tail shifted, sweeping over Sara's nose. It was so soft and fluffy, it tickled. "Hey, get your plume off my face, Plume," Sara said, the long hair brushing her lips as she spoke.

Plume came back around, kneading Sara's chest now. Then, the kitten kissed her on the nose a second time before laying down and yawning.

"Oh, is it time for us both to nap now?" Sara said with delight.

The kitten closed her eyes and Sara slid her hand out from under the sheet to stroke the kitty's back and caress under her jaw. Plume purred, and when Sara's hand got tired petting the happy kitten that was nestled under her chin, they both slept.

Chapter Nine

The next day Sara was pleasantly surprised to learn she had earned a perfect score on her math homework, and she'd also replied with the correct answer every time she'd been called on in English, Science, and American History. During keyboarding, she'd typed more words per minute than any of the other students, even nine more words than Lauren Brimes, who grumbled aloud when Mrs. Gore announced the final tally.

Even the bus isn't looking bad today, she mused before boarding. With a breath of happiness, she walked down the aisle of the school bus, her book bag held out in front, and her face forming the trace of a shy smile. Her ankle suddenly struck a rigid obstacle and she lost her balance. She tumbled forward, the stuffed bag the only thing preventing her face from slamming into the floor of the dirty bus. With the other students on the bus laughing, Sara glanced back and saw someone's leg slide out of the aisle, back behind a seat. Up in the seat,

Lauren smirked down at her before facing forward to present an innocent look for the driver.

What's with this school? Sara wanted to scream out loud but knew there wasn't anyone on the bus that would take her side, so she literally bit her tongue to keep quiet. Now that the initial shock had worn off, she smarted in a couple of places, a throbbing pain in her wrist and the aching reminder of the gymnastics injury in her neck. She struggled to her feet. There wasn't supposed to be any bullying allowed in school or on the buses.

She found a seat next to little Jimmy, who almost always kept his head down, and together they rode the bus home in silence. The extremely popular Lauren seemed to have it out for her, and no one in his or her right mind was going to interfere with the school's most popular girl. Sara suspected that if she told on Lauren the other students would turn on her even more viciously, beyond the silent treatment she was already getting from most of them.

The bus let her off and roared away. Sara turned her back on anyone who might be watching from the departing bus's windows and began to cry. Why hadn't any of the kids helped her or asked her if she was all right after Lauren had tripped her? The bus driver had to have seen her fall but didn't ever ask if she was okay. Instead, they'd laughed at her, rewarding Lauren for her mean behavior and dangerous prank. She wouldn't go back tomorrow. She'd take the day off and stay home with Plume...

Then she remembered what had happened to class delinquent Jeffrey Harris when he'd skipped school.

The school called his parents, and he'd gotten suspended and in big trouble. *So what?* she thought. With cruel kids like Lauren, Donna, and Zoe hounding her she was already in big trouble. Maybe it would be best to tell her mom what happened. Mom would understand...wouldn't she? Maybe Mom could give her advice about how to handle the situation, tell her something that would magically make Lauren and those who followed her to stop picking on her.

Mom probably couldn't help, but Sara had to give it a try as long as her mom promised she would not call the principal. She let herself in and walked right past Lincoln. She washed and went to her bedroom, shivering already as if she were about to snuggle with her pillow and cry until the sheets were wet.

The sudden thought she needed to feed the pets swung her away from the mattress, and then Plume shot out from beneath the bed and nipped her ankle.

"Ow! Oh, you wanna play?" Sara said, suddenly silly.

She played with Plume for a long time, amazed at how high the kitty jumped after the squeaky-mouse-on-a-string toy without any sort of running start.

The front door opened and shut. Josh was home from his drama class, which he always seemed so enthusiastic about. He'd gotten a role as someone called Harvey Johnson in the school's upcoming production of *Bye Bye Birdie,* and now he was walking around like *he* was the cat's meow. Smiling at Plume's loving face and her own private humor, Sara dropped the cat toy and left her room.

In the kitchen Josh glanced up from the folded newspaper on the counter, and she checked his demeanor for how receptive he might be to her problems, specifically her lousy situation at school.

"How's it going, Harvey?" she said, teasing her brother with his stage name, easing her way into more serious talk.

Josh stood, arching his spine back, and then theatrically he placed the back of his hand against his temple and said, "Working with such amateurs is sooooo beneath me. Dennis Dileo is the lead and he delivers his lines with the passion of a dry sponge, while Carrie Flowers is as ill-equipped for the role of Rosie as—" He stopped to think for a moment and Sara saw her chance!

"Josh," she said. "Will you help me with something that's been going on at school?"

Josh removed the back of his hand from his forehead. "Oh?"

"The other girls are teasing me," she said without hesitation. "How do I get to them to stop?"

Her brother looked her in the eye for a long, sad moment and said, "You're asking me?"

She glanced down at Plume who gazed up at her from beside the counter. "Yeah. You must have done something right to actually have stuff to do with people."

"Oh, I follow what you're asking me, Sear Bear." That was Josh's kid sister name for her, and she hated it mostly because he didn't pronounce the second "a" in "Sara," but she didn't interrupt. "Get active in something," Josh said. And then he shrugged and took his books and a can of diet soda with him as he strode down the hallway. "And talk to Mom. She's lived through all the girly stuff before."

Sara was dumbfounded. "I'll do that," she said to herself. She heard his door shut, meaning he wasn't to be disturbed.

Plume meowed and Sara bent down to lift her up. She carried the kitten into the hall and knocked on Josh's door. He answered two seconds later, peering at her through the partially opened door. "Yeah?"

"Feed your dog. I didn't do it yet."

Through the crack in doorway, she saw him frown, but then he nodded before shutting the door.

Off the hook from having to feed Lincoln, Sara shut herself up in her room. Plume joined her on the bed, and Sara stroked the kitten until she stopped kneading her, closed her eyes, and purred.

Suddenly Plume spun and bit her on the hand. Sara cried and twisted herself, and the kitten leapt off her onto the floor in one graceful bound. Sara sat up and checked her hand. The kitten hadn't been able to draw blood yet, but that was a painful bite regardless.

Tiny sharp teeth trying hard to puncture her skin. *Or maybe she wasn't really trying to wound me?* She checked for Plume and found her in the corner of the room, near the exit, regarding her.

Sara stared into Plume's eyes. They were yellow eyes with brown elliptical centers. From the shadow where the kitten sat her eyes seemed to become darker, like a hunter's or predator's eyes, and as Sara continued to stare into the kitten's eyes a thought occurred to her.

"You want to play? That's it, isn't it, you little wild thing?" She entered the hall.

The kitten scooted after her and then leapt. Sara could only gasp in appreciation at the height Plume achieved. The kitty climbed to about chest level. She couldn't believe the young cat could jump so high.

She swung the mouse on the string toward Plume again. This time Plume ignored it. Sara pulled the line in and that's when Plume went for it—sneakily. The kitten snagged the mouse out of the air, in a dazzling display of acrobatics, and yanked the kitty fishing pole right out of Sara's hands.

The front door opened again and Sara craned her neck to look down the hall. Her mom was home and Plume trotted toward the outside world.

"Mom, quick shut the door! She'll try to get out!"

Danielle Massey closed the door in time and stared down at Plume. "Have you been a good kitty?"

"No," Sara answered. "She hasn't. She bit me, she scares me the way she stares at me sometimes, and she just tried to escape."

"Sounds like a cat to me," Mom said, staring at the newspaper Josh had been reading. Mom was big on them not spending a lot of time online and on their phones. Sara didn't mind, but what she did mind was how no one in the world, not even Mom or Josh, ever looked her in the eyes.

"But that's just it, Mom," she said loudly. "This cat isn't like other cats."

Mom looked up. "How would you know? We've never had a cat before."

"Why haven't we?"

"Because we have enough problems...but since you promised this one a home, you've committed yourself to the responsibility, so take care of her."

"Mom?"

"Yes?" Sara's mother must've heard something in her voice and gave Sara her full attention. She reached over and ran her fingers through Sara's curly hair. "What's up, babe?"

Sara spoke slowly, making sure she told her mother only what she wanted her to know. "A few girls are teasing me at school and it hurts."

"Who?"

Sara shook her head. "I don't know what to do." She looked for Plume but the kitty wasn't in the kitchen.

"Tell me who they are. I'll report them, the school will talk to them and their parents and—"

"No, Mom," Sara interrupted. "That won't work. Things will only get worse at school." She looked into her mother's eyes. "Trust me on this. Can you just tell me what to do?"

"Get active in the school or somewhere else," her mother said.

"What can *I* do?"

"You can do a lot of things, just maybe not gymnastics or cheerleading."

"Why not?"

"Because of the risk involved, right?"

Sara nodded because she knew her mother was right. She had to think of something else. She staggered toward her room, Plume appearing from out of nowhere and trotted past her in expectation for some petting. The almost mythical bushy, orange-and-brown-ringed tail disappeared as the kitten pawed open the door and disappeared into Sara's bedroom. "Thanks, Mom. I think you just gave me an idea…"

"Sara, tell me who—"

"No, Mom," Sara called back as she opened the door to her bedroom. "I will not tell you the names of the girls teasing me. Not yet." She shut the door behind her, locked it, and joined Plume on the bed.

The kitten was demanding. She walked around the house like she owned the place, but for some reason other than Plume's fluffy fur, Sara loved her kitty. When she was with Plume, time did not seem to matter. Nothing seemed to matter.

Plume bit Sara's arm and jumped down from the bed. Sara scooted to the edge so she could watch the kitty's activities. Plume paced the room, checking for anything curious. She explored everywhere, under the bed, up on all the furniture, and finally leapt from the dresser onto the bed, startling Sara.

"Don't act like you're going to pounce on me like a tiger," Sara scolded the kitten. With her fingers she stroked the sides of Plume's face. Plume closed her eyes as Sara pet her. "It scares me when you do that… Oh, what should I do, Princess Plume?" Sara asked her kitten.

When Sara stopped stroking her, the kitten opened her eyes, suddenly alert. She sprang and in one stride was airborne, over the side of the bed…before landing on her feet. Sara slid across the mattress for a better look and saw her kitten dancing across the floor laterally in play, her back arched, eyes wild.

"Ha!" Sara blurted. "That's hilarious. A kitty dance!" She got down from the bed, left the room, and shut the door behind her. From the hall she retrieved the mouse-on-a-string toy and returned to her room.

With the door locked again, Plume performed amazing feats of agility, leaping high without a running start, sailing through the air and twisting into position for a strike. It seemed to Sara that Plume wanted her to play more, to move around, to be curious, to take chances.

She raised the mouse again and Plume shot up after it, flipping in midair to bat at the bait, tumbling and twisting only to land on her feet.

The answer to what she must do came to Sara and she blinked, watching Plume leap after the toy again. People were telling Sara she shouldn't do all the things that would make her happy. Through her wild gazes and her showing off about how high she could jump, yet land on her paws, Plume was telling Sara she could do these things if she took a risk and practiced harder than ever.

Chapter Ten

Sara hooked the higher of the two bars and paused, thinking through her dismount. Something felt wrong but she went ahead anyway, raising her legs, good form, toe to toe, thigh to thigh, swinging her legs with a jerk of her hips. And then the dismount, dizziness, and a crunching sound and shocking pain in her neck, followed by a strange taste in her nose and mouth... Her body jerked and then went limp.

She awoke, her heart beating wildly, her eyes flickering, her breath short and coming out in pants.

She'd had the dream again, reliving her collar-breaking, neck-fracturing fall during the youth competition in Charlotte two years ago. The recurrence of this real-life nightmare rekindled Sara's pain and fear, both which had lived on to torture her. She'd been in traction for a short while, her head and limbs elevated, and then the hospital nurses had lowered her down to the mattress and the pain had been excruciating. They'd given her pills which lessened the intense pain to a distant ache but returned full-force whenever the drug wore off. Now that she no longer took the pills, the aches came back from time to time.

She glanced at the digital clock on her bedside table. The alarm was set to go off in four minutes, at six-thirty. *Might as well get up*, she told herself and rolled out of bed. She checked for Plume and then, still in her nightgown, entered the hall.

Thursday, she thought padding into the bathroom where she brushed her teeth. *What do I have on Thursday?*

Math, as always, and English, she tried to think of whether today was an A day or a B day. The nightmare used this indecision to creep back into her mind.

With the crunching, cracking sound of the fall in her ears again, Sara turned from the mirror and spat into the sink. She'd planned to walk over to Percyville Center on Saturday and march through the front doors of Phoenix Gymnastics and sign up for lessons as soon as possible. Now, she wasn't so sure she could go through with it.

When she'd fallen on her neck, unable to complete the tumble and dismount, she'd fractured a vertebrae and broken her collarbone. She knew she should be grateful she could walk and move her head and neck again but she couldn't be entirely grateful. The near-crippling injury had stolen her dream of competing in the Olympics. This ambitious dream had been a sacred and long-held one, one she never talked about with her mother, even after watching the U.S. gymnastics finals on TV when she'd been five years old. She wanted what those older girls on TV possessed, great skill and confidence. The dream she'd had to someday compete in the

Olympics was just as much about love of the sport as it was about any type of near-celebrity-like recognition and fame.

Frightened or not, big risk or exaggerated, she needed to know whether she had the right stuff. The doctor told her mother and her that one more hit on her spine could possibly put her in a wheelchair, or worse. The physical therapists advised her never to get on the bars again, the sport was too dangerous. She gave herself one last look in the mirror, her tangled mess of hair even more so from its bangs knotting together in the night.

What do I have to lose? She let out a huff and opened the bathroom door.

Plume met her in the hall, trotting in front of Sara's feet. The kitten rubbed her ankles, her puffy feathery tail wrapping around Sara's leg. Sara tiptoed around the kitten and entered the kitchen.

A box of sugar-frosted, blueberry toaster pastries sat beside the toaster. Sara grabbed a plate from the cabinet and when she turned back toward the pastry box Plume was on top of the counter, sniffing the sugary sweetness beneath the cardboard and wrappers.

"Dang, how did you get up here so fast?" Sara said. She glanced down to the linoleum floor. The kitty had just jumped three and a half feet in one bound and she was only weeks old. *Imagine when she gets older...*

Sara paused and the cat nudged her wrist with her whiskered snout.

Despite the risks, the agile and flexible cat would try death-defying feats over and over again.

"Saturday," Sara said aloud. "In two days I'm going to walk into Phoenix Gymnastics and get it back."

"Get what back, hon?" Danielle Massey said entering the kitchen. She wore blue jeans and a light sweater. Like the rest of the family, she was headed out for the morning, to manage the local coffee shop, Main Avenue Café.

Before answering her mother, Sara thought for a long moment. "My courage," she said finally. "I'll start by getting that back first."

Chapter Eleven

A black limousine invaded Sara's neighborhood, the long car circled the block where Sara and her family lived. Walking the short distance from her bus stop, she watched the limo as it passed slowly. Limousines never came to this part of town and Sara wondered if the driver had taken a wrong turn off the main road. She'd noticed a few things when it passed her on the sidewalk, closer than she would have liked. The license plate had been a Washington, D.C., tag with the word 'diplomat' above the number. A diplomat was someone important, wasn't it? When she opened the storm door, the mysterious car passed again. She looked back but couldn't see any of the car's occupants through the limo's dark tinted windows. When the car disappeared around the turn, Sara grabbed the hidden key from Mom's hiding place near the door and let herself in.

Lincoln greeted her and cocked his head forward and barked. She wheeled around...nothing behind her...so she quickly shut the door, making sure to lock it. "What's the matter, boy?" she said to the collie. He barked again, less excited this time.

"Hungry?" Sara asked, walking toward the pantry where Lincoln's food was stored. She filled his bowl with two scoops, moistened the kibbles in the sink and let it sit on the counter. Taking her books to her room, she passed the phone and saw the answering machine blinking. Her mother usually checked messages, but this time she felt anxious, like it might be an important call to listen to. Something about the limousine had unnerved her. She hit play and recognized the hesitant voice instantly: Mrs. Douglas, the woman who had given her Plume.

"Danielle, uh, this is Phyllis from Round Hill Farm. Um, a man called today. He said he was from Turkey, some kind of former Sultan. He wants to interview you about the kitten you got from us. Says it is a very interesting breed of cat from his homeland. Anyway, I didn't give him your name, but call me if you want to talk to him. He said he's willing to pay a lot of money for information about this cat."

The message ended and Sara leaned into her bedroom and tossed her book bag against the wall. On the way to the bathroom the thought struck her how odd the phone message had been. The information Mrs. Douglas left on the answering machine worried her, and she wasn't sure why. As Sara washed her hands, Plume appeared on the rim of the bathtub, her tail straight in the air and swaying all the way up to its feather-like tip.

"What are you doing?" Sara said to the kitten. "Are you licking the dirty water from the tub again?"

Plume mewed and cocked her head. Sara scratched the kitten's temple.

"And the sink," Sara said. "I bet you had a good drink from that. You probably put your mouth under the faucet again."

Plume leapt onto the toilet and purred. Fortunately, the lid had been down.

Sara stroked the kitten from head to soft plush tail. "You have such an amazing tail, Plume." Sara squeezed her kitten's tail softly until she gently touched bone and let go. She petted Plume as the kitty stretched on the toilet lid and closed her eyes. Sara heard the sound of her brother closing the front door.

Josh came right to the bathroom. "What are you doing?" he asked, staring from Sara to the kitten.

"Petting my cat. How was school?"

"All right," he said with a sigh. "Hey, can you pet her somewhere else? I have to—"

"I get it," she interrupted, picked up Plume and brought her to her bedroom.

She shut the door behind her and opened her schoolbooks. Sara worked on her homework and studied for quizzes until it was dinnertime.

Over a chicken and pasta meal, Sara's mother said, "There's a man coming for dessert tonight."

They didn't usually have visitors. "Who?" Sara and Josh said at the same time.

Danielle Massey hesitated. She sighed and finally said, "I'm not sure I'm doing the best thing for this family, but I think I am."

Mom didn't normally hesitate this much when she spoke, Sara thought. *What is this all about?*

Mom continued, "But this man offered us one-thousand dollars just to come and see our cat tonight. He said he wanted 'the privilege' of seeing our cat."

"Why?" Josh said. "To measure the fatness of its doofus tail?"

Sara shot her brother an angry look and then said, "Yeah, why, Mom?"

"The man coming is the descendant of a Turkish Sultan and he says this breed of cat, uh, the kind of cat that Plume is, or the bloodline Plume belongs to, is very, very rare."

"I knew it!" Sara said with glee. But then she wondered if this man who knew so much about the cat wasn't coming to try and claim Plume as his own.

"This is garbage," Josh said, and he fed a piece of chicken to Lincoln who was begging. "No, not your cooking, Mom. This bull about Plume being a special breed of cat."

"I believe it," Sara said. "Mom, when is he coming?"

"Right after your brother helps me with dishes."

"Aw, Mom," Josh bellowed.

Sara giggled and took her plate to the sink and placed it inside. Smirking at her brother, she took a spoon from the kitchen drawer, and a half-eaten can of cat food from the refrigerator and went to feed Plume.

The silly looking man who later came to the door—at least, Sara thought he looked silly—was named Orkhan Hamid. On his head he wore a headdress of some Eastern tradition, like a Turkish prince maybe. She didn't know. It was a long, white shroud cloth that had been folded and rolled in a bubble-like design upon his head. A large birthmark shaped like an almond peeked out from beneath it. The rest of him was covered in golden silk slacks, silk shirt, silk vest, silk robe that extended down to his knees. On his feet, he wore a pair of shiny snakeskin slippers, dyed blood red. Except for his white pillowed headdress and frightening slippers, Mr. Hamid wore mostly gold.

"Welcome, Mr. Hamid," Mom said, welcoming the stranger into their home.

Sara was surprised when Mr. Hamid extended his hand to shake.

She shook the Turk's hand and he held her hand in his own, and said, "You are blessed with the possession of this sacred cat." His dark, piercing eyes held her in a grip more powerful than his handshake. "I anxiously await the opportunity to tell you about how much it means to me."

He let go of her hand and then greeted Sara's brother. Shaking off a sudden dizziness, Sara followed the others to sit at the kitchen dinner table. There, Sara's mom poured everyone drinks, Mr. Hamid accepting black tea.

Finally, when Sara's mom settled into her chair, she said, "So, Mr. Orkhan Hamid, what can we do for you?"

While staring into Danielle Massey's eyes, Mr. Hamid slid a slip of paper across the table. Sara's mom looked down. As far as Sara could tell, it was a check, already signed.

"What is it?" Mom said.

Orkhan Hamid said, "It is a check payable to you and your family, as promised, in the amount of one-thousand American dollars. Uh, may I see the animal? Is it here?"

Mrs. Massey stared down at the check, not yet touching it, and Sara could tell that her mother, too, was attempting to avoid Mr. Hamid's strange eyes.

Mom looked up. "Yes, the cat is here. Sara, where is Plume?"

Sara pushed back her chair and stood. "It's a she, Mr. Hamid, and she's probably in my room."

She dared to glance back into his dark eyes, and he met her gaze and said, "Oh, so you truly are the cat's chosen one?"

A moment of lightheadedness, and then Sara shook her head and said, "Yeah, isn't it great?"

Avoiding further eye contact with Mr. Hamid, she walked to her room, still slightly dizzy, and found Plume on the mattress, nestled against her pillow.

"Hi, Princess Plume," she said, waking the kitten. "You have a visitor."

Sara scooped up her kitten and returned to the kitchen.

The four of them moved into the family's small, more comfortable dining room, with Plume in Sara's lap. A man in his late thirties, Mr. Hamid had scary, hypnotizing eyes, but she reminded herself it was the kitten he now gazed upon. As he spoke, she would only look at her cat. She held Plume in her arms and stroked her under the chin as she listened to Mr. Hamid's thickly accented voice.

"Let me go back to the beginning," he said, leaning forward in his chair. Dessert was strawberry cheesecake and home-baked cookies. Hamid hadn't touched the cookie he'd politely accepted. "It is too complicated unless I tell you the whole story," he said.

Plume wanted to get down, to leave the table, but Sara held her. Like Mr. Hamid she'd ignored her dessert, and she wondered if a little cheesecake might convince Plume to stay longer. She plucked a piece from her slice and offered it to the kitten. Plume turned and licked her fingers with her prickly tongue and Sara giggled.

"Many centuries ago," Mr. Hamid said, his eyes on the cat, "a great flood drowned my homeland. The leader of my people back then built an ark and on it his men placed a variety of animal species and included two cats."

"Are you serious?" Sara said, but closed her mouth when Mom gave her a stern look.

He continued, "These two cats were something like the miraculous specimen in your daughter's arms, Mrs. Massey. A purer breed than the cat your daughter calls Plume, but this kitten has all the markings. I would like to ask you some questions about the cat's behavior, but later. So, the ark with the zoo aboard has these two cats, one male, one female, and when the ark settles and the sea recedes, the humans on the ark settle near the Turkish river Van."

Mr. Hamid raised his hand nobly and took a sip from the cup of tea. He made a strange face as if something wasn't right, and quickly changed his face again, into a smile. "This kind of cat, as you probably have noticed, likes the water. It descended from a breed that swam in the lake, caught fish in its bare claws, followed one person around only, not anyone else. Loyal yet wild!" he roared and smacked his hand down on the table, rattling the full cup of tea on a saucer in front of him. They all looked at him, mouths agape, and he continued his story. "This breed, the Turkish Van Cat, became a favorite of my family. We were Sultans and they were the Sultans' cats."

"This is so interesting," Sara's mom said.

Josh made himself known. "Keep going, Mr. Hamid. This is quite some tale, you know what I mean? Get it? Tail?"

"Josh!" Mom yelled. "Don't be insulting."

Orkhan Hamid smiled and raised his hand to get their attention. "Please, we should stay on the topic of why I am here," he said with respectful authority. "My great-great-grandfather was the rightful last Sultan of Turkey. He had, uh—how do you Americans say?—a kennel of pure-bred cats. My father told me he remembered his grandfather touring the world, competing in cat shows, always trying to buy the most beautiful and exotic cats of the world. He always said his Turkish Van Cats were his most cherished prizes, and they brought him luck, success, and great fortune. And then one day Great-Great-Grandfather's empire began to crumble under the might of the young rising Mehmed heir. In an attempt to change his fortune my great-great-grandfather, the rightful Sultan Orkhan the Third, journeyed to America in 1924 to find supporters and show off his Silver-Point Persians and reveal his rare and prized Turkish Van Cat. But before he could return to power as he had planned, Hamid saw his most prized cat of all escape from the show grounds at a place called Westmoreland. The soul of my great-great-grandfather, the rightful Sultan, was crushed. Soon after, even the rival sultan family of Mehmed was removed from power and the great Sultans were no more. The rest is history," Orkhan Hamid added sadly.

"Westmoreland?" Mom cut in. "Morven Park in Leesburg! That's where they've always had cat shows. They still do. It's ten miles from here."

Mr. Hamid nodded. "Yes, it is. What I don't understand is how this kitten of yours managed to stay so true to the breed. I wonder if a male Turkish Van Cat is not somehow also in the area, but enough of that... My great-great-grandfather's cat ran away before the show, and his fortunes turned for the worse. Never again did an Orkhan rule in my homeland, and since that time, my family has suffered greatly."

Sara stared at Mr. Hamid, no longer fearing his eyes. He was looking inward, remembering, so she didn't think he could hypnotize her. Without looking at her, he said, "Does the cat like to climb and swim around in the toilet bowl?"

"Yup," Sara said, no longer frightened or suspicious of the visitor. Mr. Hamid was interested in the wonderful uniqueness of Plume, and he drew her attention with his passionate knowledge of the history of Plume's kind.

"I don't believe this," Josh said. He got up from the table, and in his gangly teenage way, swayed off to his room.

"I'm sorry about him," Mom said.

Mr. Hamid waved the matter off. "The blood in this particular cat coursed through the veins of Turkish Van Cats that have been part of my family for centuries!" he said angrily. He rapped his chest.

Mrs. Massey gave a start, and Plume tensed in Sara's arms. Things were turning, and Mr. Hamid was scaring her again.

He said, "I want this cat, and I am prepared to pay excellently for it. Uh, may I hold her?" Mr. Hamid reached for her, and Sara hopped out of the chair with Plume hissing.

"Sorry," Sara said, not meaning it. "I guess she's kind of protective of me." She now stood a safe seven feet away from Mr. Hamid, nearly in the hall.

"No need to apologize," he said, studying their house more carefully now. Then, from the breast pocket of his robe he produced his checkbook and a pen. He wrote out a second check, signed it, and slid it across the table toward Sara's mom.

Mom's jaw dropped. Then, quickly she recovered and yelled, "Josh, get out here now. Family decision time!"

"I'll get him," Sara said, thinking quickly. She brought Plume with her and pushed the kitten into her bedroom. Then, she knocked on Josh's door. "Josh, get out here. Family business. And you better vote the way I want you to. Plume is part of the family now!"

Out in the dining room, Mr. Hamid said, "Five thousand American dollars for the animal you know as Plume."

"She's not for sale!" Sara barked, her trust of Orkhan Hamid completely gone. "No amount of money…"

"Ten," Danielle Massey said, haggling with the Turkish stranger.

Sara gasped. "Mom!"

Josh returned to the dining room. "I think you're an imposter," he said to Mr. Hamid, and Sara wondered if her brother didn't have something here. The proclaimed great-great-grandson of a long-dead Turkish Sultan, who had been the last of his kind. At first Sara had felt kind of sad for him, but now—

"Mother, Plume is not for sale," she said. "I don't care how much the house is breaking down around us."

As Sara watched, her mother bit her lip. Then, Mom swallowed and said, "My daughter is right, Mr. Hamid, our cat is not for sale."

Mr. Hamid withdrew his checkbook again. He wrote this check out for ten-thousand U.S. dollars.

"Oh, Sara, get me a cigarette," Danielle Massey said faintly.

"No, Mom!" Sara hollered. She spun to face her brother. "How do you vote, Josh?"

Josh turned to face Mr. Hamid wearing a frown of disgust. "Hit the road, phony...and without the cat. Your check is probably no good anyway."

Sara dared a glance at Mr. Hamid. With his hypnotic eyes he stared at her brother. Josh's eyes opened wide, and for the first time he appeared slightly afraid. "You're a con man. Some kind of cheat," her brother said, this time with hesitation.

Mr. Hamid squinted in a moment of indecision. Josh had insulted him again, and Sara froze, wondering if Mr. Hamid was about to strike her brother.

"I will go," the Turk said, standing up. "My driver waits." He glanced around before snatching back the last two checks he'd made out to Sara's family. He left the thousand-dollar check, though, which at least showed he had been true to his promise to pay just to see Plume.

At the door, Orkhan Hamid, the self-professed great-great-grandson of the last Turkish Sultan, sniffed and said somberly, "I will do anything to have that cat back in my family's possession."

He wiped a tear from his eye, and then opened the door and left, while Sara's mom rubbed her palms over her face in regret. "That last check was for ten-thousand dollars," she said, her voice slowly emphasizing the amount. She pretended to sob.

"Mom?" Sara said tentatively. "Please tell me you're not thinking about selling my cat."

"No, I'm not," Danielle Massey replied. "The house can wait." She swallowed a last bit of regret. "Plume is too important to you."

Chapter Twelve

That night Sara headed into the bathroom to prepare for bed, her mind still on the mysterious Turkish visitor and his bizarre story about Plume's ancestry. If what Orkhan Hamid said was true, a lot about Plume made sense. The kitten's fluffy, plume-like tail, her odd pattern of markings...you could say Plume's marking had no pattern at all...the kitten's athleticism, her sweet meow, and her surprising attraction to water.

And her loyalty to one person.

Sara lowered the toilet seat...and just in time because out of nowhere Plume leapt up and walked around the rim. "Hey!" Sara said. "It's my turn. You have your own bathroom by the back door."

Plume mewed and walked back around the seat in the other direction, her feathery tail tickling Sara's arm. Sara picked the kitten up—Plume felt heavier now, like she was growing. And she looked bigger, too.

"Why do you like water so much?" she said, placing her cat on the floor. Sara sat down and stared at Plume.

In response, Plume let out a squeak and then leapt up onto the rim of the bathtub. She looked into the big basin and then hopped down inside. Sara let her kitty wander around in there as she washed her hands and brushed her teeth. She was just putting her toothbrush back in its holder when Plume appeared suddenly on the rim of the sink.

Sara's mouth opened wide. The kitten had just leapt four feet at least, and stopped on a dime to easily collect her balance on the narrow sink rim. Plume wasn't afraid of anything. She chased, pawed, and terrorized Lincoln, a collie who was ten times her size, she leapt and visited any part of the house she wanted to, no matter how Sara and her family tried to keep some spots off-limits, and she showed no sign of fear of water or anything else for that matter.

"I wish I could be more like you, Plume," Sara said. "Not ashamed of who I am and not afraid of anything." She plucked Plume from the sink and carried her into her bedroom. Placing Plume down on the mattress beside her, Sara lay back thinking.

She dreaded tomorrow more than she had ever dreaded a day before, because tomorrow she faced a decision she didn't yet know the answer to. At a time when everyone she trusted was telling her to get more involved, find something she was passionate about, the one thing she *was* passionate about posed a number of risks.

Gymnastics... and risks like falling from the bars or beam could quite possibly put her in a wheelchair.

Plume nudged Sara's nose with her wet, pink snout. Purring, the kitten spread out on Sara's chest and began to lick her paw.

"I know," Sara said. "You're telling me to talk to the paw, I get it."

The kitten licked her paw, tugging on the tufts of white fur sticking out between her padded toes. She noticed something new about this breed of cat every time she stared at Plume.

Wait, Sara thought. *Now I'm starting to act as if I believe Plume really is one of those Turkish Van Cats.* Despite her initial excitement and the flicker of joy in her heart over the news her kitten was a rare and exotic breed, the chances of this all being true were still slim in her mind.

Mom had done an Internet search on possible sultan families named Hamid and found the name as common in Turkish history as Johnson or Jackson was in American. She did confirm Turkish Sultans loved cats of all kinds and kept the animals upon the royal grounds as well as inside their palaces.

A more telling finding was that of a young fifteenth-century prince named Orkhan the First, labeled the Pretender, but that had been all the information the mysterious passage had provided. The Internet had no record of Sultan Orkhan the Third having ever visited the United States with a prized cat.

Suddenly Plume caught her attention when the kitten stopped licking her paw and cocked her head to stare above Sara. She saw the muscles in the cat's haunches flex and then Plume soared in an arc toward her head. Sara shut her eyes and her hands came up to protect her face, but Plume only trotted over her right shoulder, using Sara as a step on her way to walk the narrow beam of the bed board.

"Oh, my gosh," Sara said because even in anxiety she never took the Lord's name in vain. Just because her new cat had just leapt over her head, using her shoulder as a trampoline, she still didn't have an excuse to curse. Cursing brought bad luck and she didn't need any more bad luck.

She knelt at the foot of the bed and prayed, not caring now if the other kids at school acted like it was uncool. Besides she was alone now and feeling alone, she needed to talk to the head honcho right now. She needed guidance. She needed someone other than a cat to tell her what to do.

During one of her manic, upbeat periods she'd decided tomorrow would be the day she would show up for a lesson at the gymnastics school in the center of Percyville called Phoenix Gymnastics.

She knew a few of the girls from school would be there, and she knew for a fact that Zoe Fallon, one of Lauren Brimes's two bookends, practiced there—so she wasn't too optimistic about feeling welcome at the gym. *God, please help me make the right decision. I don't know what to do.*

Her elbows on the mattress, she begged God to give her the strength to persist when so many others seemed to want to prevent her happiness.

Plume had rolled over on her back, nuzzling Sara's hand in delight as Sara stroked the kitten under her ear. Then the kitten accidentally rolled right off the bed. Sara gasped but saw Plume miraculously land on her splayed feet, a little scared but safe.

"That was some dismount," Sara said, and confidently Plume stretched and turned her head toward her and meowed sweetly, but with an energy that lifted Sara's mind and soul.

To Sara's delight, Plume jumped back on the bed. Sara shut her eyes and welcomed sleep. Together she and Plume slept soundly. However, just before awakening, Sara fell from the bars again, injuring her neck and breaking her collar bone. Opening her eyes, she started to pant in relief. She felt her heart hammering inside her chest and she was sweating.

It was impossible to put this terrible incident behind her. Her repeated nightmares were not merciful, and she awoke anxious and without confidence often. This one had shaken her as such nightmares always did, and this time so terrifyingly that she'd felt the pain all over again. How could she move past it when it happened so randomly several times every month?

She could recall each break. The crunching sound of her bones breaking after her forehead, shoulder, and knee collided with the mat. Plume had left, probably due to Sara's restless jolts while sleeping. Wasn't there someone who would talk with her? Guide her? God usually wasn't a direct talker. She would have to look for signs from her daily life.

Maybe if she just lay in bed a little longer the answer would come. She pulled the bed sheet over her head like a shroud.

She felt a slight vibration on the mattress followed by the weight of paws on her arm and then chest. Plume jumped on top of her, and through the sheerness of the sheet Sara saw Plume's shadowy feline head sniffing her, probably curious why she could smell and feel human but not see human.

"I'm down here, Plume." Sara giggled. "Under the sheet." The kitten acted confused and jumped down from the bed.

"Hey, you're no fun!" she said, throwing the sheet aside and leaning to check to see where Plume had gone. The kitten was pacing at the foot of Sara's sloppily covered dresser. The dresser was lined with perfumes, piggy banks, and photos of her mom, brother, and Lincoln.

"Hey!" Sara said to Plume. "We need to get a picture of you up there."

Plume jumped but this time missed her mark. Her paws slipped off the dresser top and her hind legs reached for something as the cat twirled, flipped, and then—

Landed on her feet.

Of course. Cats always landed on their feet.

But humans?

Determined, Plume leapt again, knocking over the framed photo of Lincoln before gaining a foothold on top of the bureau. The cat investigated, sniffing Sara's hairbrush and comb, her dazzling tail reflecting in the mirror. Plume had risked another jump, Sara thought. *Right after a fall.* Maybe that was what this special cat was trying to tell her.

Risks were always necessary.

She got out of bed and got dressed. She was going down to Phoenix Gym on Main Street right now, even if she had to walk.

Because it was Saturday, a non-school day, there would be nothing to stop her except her own fears. She just had to get down there, register, and start. And then a thought hit her. To participate in anything, she needed her mother's permission and signature. From her room, she went looking for her mom and followed the clanging sounds of pots and pans and the scent of bacon frying. Mom was with Josh in the kitchen.

"Hon, you want some eggs?" Danielle Massey asked.

Sara nodded and then tentatively said, "Um, Mom, I want to try gymnastics again."

As she waited, a tear pooled in her eye and rolled down her cheek. It had taken her two years of recovery, physical therapy, and, most of all, emotional healing to reach this decision. And now that she'd reached it, a fit of crying...and of dread...took over. She was certain what her mom's answer would be.

The kitchen went silent, except for the sound of bacon sizzling. Mom turned from the fryer to stare at her. For a long moment, her face wore a frown, but then at last she shrugged. "Sure, hon," she replied. "I know that's what you've always wanted."

Sara suppressed a cry of joy. Her mother wasn't done talking.

"But take it easy at first, okay? No high-wire act or anything like that." Mom chuckled.

Speechless, Sara gazed at her mother. She had expected Mom to give her a blunt, "No," or a lecture on the dangers of falling from the bars again.

Instead, her mom had smiled and said she could return to gymnastics.

"Sit down and have something to eat," Mom continued. "I have to be at the coffee shop by noon for the lunch shift, but I'll stop by the school beforehand and sign all the paperwork. Josh can drive his car to the gym and bring you home from there."

"Aww, Mom!" Josh protested.

Mom turned from the bacon and shot Josh a stern look. "Josh, how can you say that? You know how much this means to your sister."

Sara wiped the tears from her eyes. "Mom, I, uh." She sniffled. "I never expected you to say yes. I thought you'd be too worried I'd get hurt again."

Mom's face was soft and kind. "What? And keep you from your passion? Are you kidding me? I was wondering when you were going to ask. What made you decide now?"

"Because I'm ready," Sara said. "And—" She covered her mouth as Plume got up on the chair, put her paws on the kitchen table, and nibbled at the remainder of Danielle's Massey's breakfast. Sara pointed. "Her! She convinced me to go back."

"Shoo!" Josh said and waved his hand at the kitten who ignored him and kept eating.

"Get down from there, you breakfast burglar!" Mom cried. Sara giggled and went over, picked up her cat, and carried her from the kitchen.

Chapter Thirteen

Phoenix Gymnastics was next to Mike's Sub Sandwiches in the newly developed center of Percyville. A construction crew had demolished the antique barn and built a shopping mall. Even if Sara had wanted never to think about gymnastics again, the arrival of Phoenix Gymnastics with its large white, black, and orange sign would have been a constant reminder. She knew she couldn't move out of town, not until she was older, so she realized she had to face her fear right away. The bell over the door jingled as she walked in the front door and silence greeted her as she looked around.

No one sat at the front desk, but to Sara's right was the doorway into what appeared to be the training studio. Before she could peer in at the event in progress, a woman emerged from the studio and nodded to her. "Can I help you?"

"I'm Sara Massey," Sara answered hesitantly. "Today's my first day."

"Great. I'm Coach Jane." The woman was short and had dyed, close-cropped hair. Her skin was tan and looked as tough as leather. "We've already started."

Coach Jane cleared her throat and waved Sara toward the training wing. "You can get changed in the locker room in the back of the gym."

Embarrassed at being late, Sara followed the woman into the training studio. The floor beneath her feet was tiled with blue padded mats. The ceiling was high, accommodating the uneven bars, a set of rings, and the perfect height the girls would need to reach to perform their routines. Several girls were stretching, some of them using the bars and big exercise balls. "I thought class started at nine," she said.

"We get warmed up a half-hour before, so I expect everyone here by eight-thirty. Okay?"

Sara murmured an apology. It was about eight-fifty now. *Darn, what a terrible start.* She took her duffle bag into the girls' changing room.

Minutes later she returned to the training studio in a leotard and spandex. The other girls were huddled around Coach Jane, who looked toward her as she approached. "Everyone, this is Sara," Coach Jane said. Then, to one of the girls, she said, "Donna, why don't you help Sara stretch? The rest of you split up in twos. Keep it moving. I want a push-up station here, crunches station here, a—"

"Hi, Sara. What brings you to Phoenix?"

Sara turned to see Donna Sutherland. Why did it have to be her? She kept silent. *This is going to be hard.*

"Never mind," Donna said, when Sara didn't answer. "Get on the mats. You're down first."

With a nervous frown Sara got down on the floor into stretching position. She didn't like the way this was starting. Not at all.

She extended her legs straight in front of her and leaned forward. The idea was to touch her knees with her forehead and grasp her toes. For two years she hadn't tried and as she stretched now the tightness and pain gripped her from her hips all the way up to her neck. She moaned and was about to sit up and relax when Donna pushed down on her upper back, as a stretching partner was supposed to do, although not as hard as Donna pushed now.

"Ow," Sara let out. "Hold on," she said, expecting the bigger girl to let up.

"Can't you stretch more than that?" Donna scolded, pressing down harder.

Her eyelids clenched shut in pain, Sara wondered if Donna and the others knew about her injury she'd had when she lived in Charlotte. If Donna had learned of her injury, would she understand or try to continue pushing to hurt her? "Donna," Sara said, patting the mat. "Let go a second."

Donna rose from the mat. "What's wrong with you, Bird's Nest?"

Still seated, Sara spun to face Donna. *What was Bird's Nest? Because of my hair?* she wondered. Then she told herself to forget about whatever *Bird's Nest* meant. Instead, she had to let Donna know she'd broken a vertebra. In a whisper only Donna could hear she said, "When I was nine, I broke a bone in my spine, near my neck. I broke my collar bone, too."

Donna shrugged and looked away. "What are you doing here, then, Bird's Nest? Does the coach know this?" she said loudly enough so some of the other girls looked over.

"I'm taking up gymnastics again," Sara answered, irritated. "What's with the bird's nest thing?"

"Oh, I don't know." Donna looked away again. "Maybe it's your hair. I don't want to touch it. Stretch yourself—I'm gonna, uh, go rejoin the others." Donna trotted off, and then did a perfect cartwheel before halting next to Zoe who had been waiting for her by the uneven bars.

Oh, great, Sara thought. *My first day back and I have to start without stretching.* And now Coach Jane was assigning them to events...

"...Michelle to the vault, Donna to the unevens, and Sara to the men's rings."

With a mix of curiosity and dread, Sara walked over to an arched framework of bars. From the top beam hung two cords culminating in a pair of foam-padded rings.

"The men's rings will give you a chance to stretch without too much risk of injury," Coach Jane explained.

A short, muscular young man stood at the station. He nodded to her, shuffled beneath the rings, and slipped his hands inside them, lifting his legs off the ground. As he demonstrated how to use the rings, mainly for Sara's purposes, she glanced around to check the other stations and students there.

Zoe was just finishing her turn on the uneven bars, and seconds after her feet slapped down on the mat she received a high-five from Donna who then leapt and seized the lower bar.

As Donna's legs hooked the bar and she pumped her arms and twirled, Sara observed how strong, flexible, athletic, and talented the tall blonde girl was. Moving from low bar to high, Donna performed a series of somersaults, clenches, straddles, and then a perfect dismount.

Sara watched as Zoe clapped and stepped in to high-five her friend.

"Switch!" Coach Jane yelled, prompting the group of girls to scramble to their next station. Sara walked across the gym privately beating herself up for being late, missing any chance to stretch. Following the rotation of the other gymnasts, she stopped at the next station where a sleepy-eyed, dark-skinned young woman waited in front of the balance beam. If Sara had to guess, the woman looked to be twenty at most. Her gray sweat suit had block-letter maroon markings down the side that said VA Tech.

"Your turn," the college athlete turned instructor said without looking up. It seemed as if the girl was just starting out as an instructor, still a bit shy. "Let me know if you need any help."

Seeing that no one was in front of her, Sara turned toward the balance beam. She remembered how to get up on it. It was just a matter of whether her body could perform the feat or not. Tiptoeing beside the beam, she stretched her arches a bit and then swung a leg up over it and extended her leg muscles. She tried the other leg, and when she felt good she hopped up and sat on the bar. For a moment she was dizzy as she straddled the beam, almost tumbling over. It would take a while before she felt comfortable in the gym again.

"Hi." The shy instructor appeared by the beam, facing her with more energy in her voice than before. "I'm Sonya." The girl brushed her bangs out of her eyes and pressed her face closer. "Good so far. Need any help yet?"

Sara pivoted on her bottom and then straddled the beam. "No," she said unsteadily, as she prepared for her next move. She placed her head down on the beam and lifted one knee and placed it down, then the other. Sliding her legs back, she pinned her toes to the beam and then pressed off with her palms as if doing a push-up...one, two, and then she was on her feet, standing on the balance beam.

Her confidence waned at the next station: the uneven bars. She'd seen Zoe and Donna own these bars with such mesmerizing grace, but to her these bars represented a return to the most horrifyingly unforgettable moment of her life. When she'd failed to complete the backwards somersault and landed on her chest... If it had been her neck she would have died, the doctors had told her mom, but the broken clavicle and fractured upper vertebra had been enough to scare her away from gymnastics until now.

When her turn came she clenched the bars and hoisted herself up with Coach Jane spotting her. But with every duck of her head and every swing of her pelvis came a crack from her joints and a reminder of her injury, the arthritis it had left behind. At only eleven, Sara felt old, hobbled; unathletic. And then the anxiety hit, the fear of falling, the crunching sound of bone echoed in her memories, her dreams, from when her chest had impacted with the mats...

She did what she could, stretching, moving from high beam to low, gripping the bar and feeling it in her fingers again for the first time. She extended her legs and pointed her toes, and stretched. The thought of trying a somersault entered her brain, and she turned toward the coach.

"Go ahead," Coach said. "I've got your back."

But a sharp ache stung Sara's upper spine as if to give her warning. Suddenly short of breath, she dropped down to her feet, inhaling carefully, trying to tell herself it was all right...part of the healing process.

Days later, on those same bars, she did her first back hip circle. As weeks passed each spin got tighter and tighter until Sara dared the very dismount that had nearly crippled her. She proceeded in almost a daze, as if accepting the death that would result if she fell again. During a somersault she lost her breath, her wind sucked from her, and for a moment time slowed...

Certain she would crash, her body reacted, purely on instinct. She tucked her chin, then her arms, and grasped the flesh of her rear thighs. It wasn't perfect but she landed on her feet, actually on her heels and she flailed and stumbled until her arms came up in completion and the spotter, Coach Jane, was there to keep her upright. "You did great," the coach said. "You're taking it at your own speed. That's what we want here."

Sara lowered her arms and nodded her thanks to the head instructor. As she waited for the next station rotation. Coach Jane said, "I want you to rotate back to the rings. Work those muscles some more."

Sara smiled. This was getting better, easier. Her confidence was beginning to bloom once again. Then, with a voice that filled the gymnasium, Coach Jane shouted, "Switch!"

Using the rings, which traditionally were equipment for men, Sara lifted her body off the floor, her arms getting a workout as she swung and rotated her hips, learning how to use them all over again.

"Switch!" the coach yelled. "Donna and Zoe, the unevens, Meghan and Ileana that vault isn't getting enough work, Michelle the floor, Sara back to the beam for balance. Go!"

Sara gladly trotted back to the balance beam. She still didn't quite have it yet. Her balance. It was better but not all back yet. She noticed it mainly on her dismounts. That sense of shakiness, that ache, weakness in the joints, a slight dizziness in which she felt like she was about to collapse.

She walked on the beam, one careful step after the other, all the way to the end where she stopped and shuffled backwards, toeing the straight line behind her, following it.

"Breathe," Sonya, the Virginia Tech gymnast, told her. The young woman stood on the station's mats, watching. "Your breathing is just as much a part of your balance as your body."

Sara breathed deeply and gently, and then toe-to-heel she walked backwards over the beam.

Later that afternoon at home, she wandered into the kitchen. Josh, who'd braved the snow flurries to drive her home, was playing with his phone. Surprised to find him there instead of in his room, she paused at the refrigerator. "What's up?" she said.

"Going for big score," he mumbled without looking up from the game he played. He tapped expertly with his thumbs. "How was practice?"

"Good," she said and smiled, though Josh didn't see it.

She skipped to the bathroom, giggling as Plume shot in before she could close the door. Her muscles ached so she set the water in the shower as hot as she could stand it.

It was February and her thoughts were on how Coach Jane had told her she was nearly ready to compete. As the pellets of hot water pelted Sara's sore and exhausted body, she thought about her slow progress and the upcoming meet. The past few months had been a blur, but in that time she'd regained some of the moves she'd learned before her fall.

Still, she feared the upcoming tournament because her bones ached in constant remembrance of how she'd crashed at a similar tournament nearly two years ago. Word had spread about her background and mishap in gymnastics. Both in school and at gymnastics class she heard the whispers and a few had even asked her outright if she was the same Sara Massey who crashed chest and face-first into the mat at the 2014 Fall Fest Tournament. She closed her eyes. Hadn't she proven lately with all of her hard work and dedication that she could come back?

The iciness of the shower jolted her back to her surroundings, she wiped the water out of her eyes and adjusted the temperature as far as she could but it was lukewarm at most ... *I must have used up all the hot wa-*

ter. *How long have I been—?* A shadowy figure pressed against the outside of the shower glass. Sara shrieked. Then, she recognized Plume's face peering in and laughed. "You scared me there, little kitty." She opened the glass shower door and said, "Okay, let's see how much you really love water, Turkish Van Cat." She waited for a moment, and then the kitten trotted over and investigated the wet, steaming compartment in which Sara bathed.

"You see, I can't clean myself the same way you do with that sandpaper tongue of yours, little Princess Plume, so I have to get in here and turn on the jets."

Plume entered the reach of the cooling spray of water and didn't seem to mind either the water or the force of it. Tail up, she padded across the shower stall and rubbed Sara's leg. Astonished, Sara opened her mouth and stared down at the wet kitty below, Plume's long coat drenched and dripping, the cat now looking smaller from the water's weight. Sara could hold it in no longer and she laughed. She turned back toward the water jets, finishing her cold shower, still chuckling but moving a little faster now. She knew she'd have to be careful not to step on Plume when she washed her hair. Minutes later she finished and stepped out. Plume remained inside the shower, staring up at the shower head, probably wondering why the fun spray of water had stopped.

A breed of cat that loves water, she thought and took a towel to dry herself off. *Far out.*

Chapter Fourteen

"Hey, Bird's Nest."

Sara stopped in her tracks, dreading the worst. Donna put her hand on Sara's shoulder and Sara turned to look up at her fellow sixth grader, who was nearly a head taller than her.

Why now? Sara wanted to know. *She hasn't called me that name since the first day of practice.* She swallowed. "What?"

Donna stared at her strangely. "I respect you for coming back." She patted Sara's arm and turned to go. The bell was ringing for the next class.

"Donna," Sara said finally. She'd been tongue-tied but now she understood the importance of the moment, the need to act. "Thank you. That means a lot to me."

Donna nodded and disappeared into a throng of students waiting to turn the corner into Wing A, where many classes would start. Sara hurried off and ducked into history where Mrs. Gaffney waited by her desk. She took her seat and opened her history notebook.

What did this mean that Donna had said something nice to her all of a sudden? Was it part of some joke she and the other girls were playing on her, with no doubt Lauren behind it all? Lauren, Donna, and Zoe hadn't been teasing her lately. Although Lauren had glared at her often from across the cafeteria, staring at her so long that Sara could sense the girl's hatred, and when she turned, Lauren didn't look away as people usually did when caught staring. Zoe, on the other hand, never looked at Sara, not even when the two passed in the hall or practiced gymnastics together. Even when the two were paired by Coach Jane, Zoe couldn't be bothered to speak or look at the likes of Sara. *It's as if I don't exist to her,* Sara brooded.

But all in all things were getting better.

Zoe entered the classroom, walking right past the teacher without a glance. She sat at her usual spot by the door, put her books down flat as she always did, but then surprised Sara when she looked over. She smiled in Sara's direction before facing forward again.

Yeah, something's definitely up. Donna says something supportive in the hall and now arrogant, studious, I'm-smarter-and-better-than-you Zoe, smiles at me? They're planning something.

She thought about this throughout the whole class, and didn't listen to Mrs. Gaffney as she explained American history and the colonists' grievances with England.

Deep in thought, she slept-walked through the rest of the school day. She took the bus home, fed the dog, and went to find Plume. Gymnastics practice started in less than an hour, but she really needed to spend time with someone she trusted for a while. Someone who had given her answers to her life's mysteries before.

Asleep on Sara's bed, the cat awoke when she entered, stretched, and trotted over. Sara stroked Plume's fur, petting her fluffy tail all the way to the raccoon-like tip before returning to the cat's head. Her kitten was no longer looking like a kitten, having grown into a long animal that more resembled a weasel than a feline. Sara threw her books down and sat on the mattress with her cat. Plume nudged her waist with her curling spine and threw herself down onto her back.

Sara's fingers left the cat's temple and tentatively tried Plume's belly. Here the cat's fur was shaggier but still soft as feather down. She glided her hand down Plume's chest. Without warning, Plume attacked, latching onto Sara's wrist with her claws, although gently, and biting Sara's index finger.

"Ow!"

To this, the cat sprung to her feet and leapt down and disappeared under the bed.

"Is that any way to greet your owner and best friend?" As she swung her foot forward to get off the mattress, a paw shot out from under the bed frame. Sara moved her foot out of range and giggled. Plume was using the paw with the brown splotch on the toe to go after Sara's feet. It was Sara's favorite paw. She moved her other foot and the same paw shot out again, swiping at her heel. "Ha-ha!"

She let the cat play some more and then got up to feed Lincoln. "There's a hungry dog out there, Plume, and he probably has to go to the bathroom. He doesn't use an indoor bathroom like you." Stepping toward the door, she had to stop short when Plume trotted across the carpet right in front of her feet, cutting her off. She raised her foot high and placed it down safely as Plume cut her off again, this time from the other direction. Moving more quickly, Sara reached the door and went down the hall, glancing back. Plume was no longer following her.

Lincoln waited in the kitchen, his face full of its usual hungry anticipation this time of day. She fed him and let him out and returned to her bedroom to change for gymnastics.

Chapter Fifteen

As Sara stretched that following Saturday morning, her thoughts wandered to next week's tournament. During a practice earlier in the week, Coach Jane had given her the okay to compete again, so she'd signed up with her mom's permission as a late entry for the Cardinal Classic.

Although she was excited, her anticipation was mixed with dread as once again her mind returned to her accident two years ago in which she'd miscalculated her dismount from the asymmetric bars and crashed to the mats. She knew it would never be possible to remove the experience from her mind, but with enough practice, and some competitions, maybe she could replace the fear of the near paralyzing fall with her newfound courage and confidence. All the same, she'd decided to ease her way back into the competitive circuit by having Coach Jane spot her in some of the events.

After limbering up at the rings and floor mats, she moved to the uneven bars where the young man from the men's ring station was standing. His name was

Kyle, he was in his twenties with wavy dark brown hair, bushy eyebrows, and mischievous dark eyes. Of average height and muscular build, he wore a handsome, tight-fitting black and gold U.S. Army sweat suit that had caused her to notice him earlier. For the first time he looked at her with his lively, crazy eyes, and she couldn't look away.

"Hi, sorry I didn't introduce myself the last time I instructed here. I'm Kyle," he said with a grin. "Ready to work a bit on the unevens?"

A guy teaching me how to use the uneven bars? What in the heck is going on?

She cleared her throat. "I'm Sara. How do you know—?"

"How do I know anything about the uneven bars?" he said finishing her statement. And with that, he spun on his feet, addressed the bars and leapt up.

His hands gripped the lower bar and he swung under it, spread his legs and brought them gracefully together before lifting them straight up until his thighs tapped the bar. Using the momentum from this tap he swung back under, extending his legs behind him and thrust them into the lower bar where his body jackknifed, and with a jerk of his powerful arms he shot his lower body straight up over the bar where his legs remained perfectly erect for a moment. She watched him, her mouth agape. As he swung back down, his feet touched the lower beam before his feet slid under the bar and in a second jackknifed position he swung under the lower bar and released. Gaining height, he grasped the higher bar, turning in midair as his legs carried out, away from the equipment. The recoil brought his body back toward the bars.

Sara continued to watch in awe. She thought he was kind of cute, and his demonstration was both amazing and funny. Funny because he was a guy who, with his own sense of style, was manipulating a piece of equipment designed for females. Still clenching the upper bar, Kyle swung and let go. He seized the lower bar, knifed his legs under it and propelled himself backwards and up. He gripped the higher bar, letting go, twisting, gripping it again, and then extending, swinging the back of his legs onto the lower bar and straight up, farther until his toes touched his hands on the upper bar. He shifted behind the bar, and eyed the lower bar with concentration. Sara looked around and saw that everyone had paused to watch Kyle's unusual routine. He grunted and then dropped, his pelvis caroming off the lower bar. He somersaulted on it and flew back, managing to grasp the upper bar with his back to it. *Amazing.*

Using a backhanded grip, he did a funny orangutan arm-swinging motion along the upper bar, and Coach Jane laughed heartily and said, "Stop the aping around, Kyle, and get back to work."

Kyle smiled mischievously and dropped to the lower bar and somersaulted before hurling himself back to the upper bars where he switched his hands forward. He somersaulted again and again, and placed his feet on the bar in preparation for his dismount. His legs shot back and his thighs met the lower bar. He jackknifed over the lower bar and somersaulted to place his feet on the upper rung again. Sliding under the bar he jettisoned into an airborne somersault and landed safely on his feet.

Some of the girls behind Sara clapped and she joined in. Kyle beamed and then looked at her. "Your turn," he said. "Let me know if you need any help."

"Thanks," she said and approached the unevens. "I think I'll start with a simple routine today." She leapt to grip the lower rung. "And by that I mean *much* simpler than what you did."

"That's fine," he said. "Take it at your own speed."

She started on the mat with some reverse hollow body hold stretches, which were a little like a front bridge, only lower to ground, and involved pushing and strengthening the arms, legs, and stomach muscles.

Standing and gripping the lower rung, she pushed her upper body over the bar. These were called casts, a basic move leading to the more difficult ones she would have to perform. Arms straight, and pushing down on her shoulders, she sucked in her stomach while swinging her feet forward under the bar, toes straight. She moved her shoulders forward over the bar and pushed down while rocking her tightly pressed legs back and forward again into the bar. It was a great exercise for strengthening the key muscles and preparing for her next maneuver: the back hip circle.

With a grunt she swung her thighs against the bar and performed a slow and imperfect back hip circle, her head heavy and something in her neck cracking in resistance.

"Good," Kyle told her. "But make sure you don't throw your head back. Keep it straight."

He was right. Her body wasn't behaving as it had used to.

"I'm trying." She attempted another and once again her head felt heavy and rolled back throwing off her balance. Still, she completed the maneuver.

"Okay, drop down," Kyle said. "Let's do some chin-up pullovers to strengthen those critical muscles and keep your head from moving." He went to the corner of the gym and returned with a bright red giant exercise ball which he placed three feet from the lower bar. "Grab hold of the bar and place your heels on top of the ball." Sara did. "Now, keeping your legs together and straight, pull your chin up over the bar."

She recognized the exercise. She'd done it often, years ago as a beginner, and felt a bit discouraged that Kyle was taking her back to the basics.

As if reading her thoughts, he said, "I know this is a beginner stretch, but it's gonna help. Trust me."

He smiled at her. She smiled back as she pulled her chin over the bar. She let out a breath and tightened her stomach muscles and the muscles in her neck. Clenching the bar, she thrust her body forward and up and craned her neck so her chin touched the bar. Two.

Already her arms ached, but she managed to tilt her chin over the bar for a third chin-up.

"Breathe," Kyle reminded.

She took a breath and again tightened her stomach muscles, flexed her toes, and surged up over the bar. Four. Unable to get over the bar again, she dropped to the mat.

"Good. Now move over to the balance beam," Kyle said. "We have to keep working on your strength and getting your sense of balance back."

Her arm muscles burning, she held herself, her fingers kneading her bicep muscles. She glanced at Kyle.

I like him, but what is he, like my coach now? And is that a bad thing? He seemed to be right about most things, most recently that she didn't have her strength and balance back yet.

Next week she'd be competing. She planned to do a floor routine and then a walk on the beam, a basic routine on the unevens, and a vault, which had never given her much trouble. She knew she would indeed have to concentrate on strength and balance for the rest of practice.

Coach Jane blew her whistle and Sara approached the balance beam. She was sweating a lot and not so much from physical exertion. Her palms and soles were moist and that was not good for gymnastics. There was a knot in her chest, an almost suffocating warning she should quit right now and go home before she hurt herself again.

Another part of her wanted to push forward through the pain and anxiety to *go ahead, take a chance.* It was a part of her that had been missing since the accident, an energetic and rebellious energy. Her arms were tired but strong enough for the cartwheels she had to perform so she raised them again, planted her palms on the beam and lifted herself up into a sitting position. She shoved herself to her feet and stretched.

"Let it rip, Sara!" a girl shouted.

Sara paused in her ballerina stretch. The voice had been Donna's voice.

Donna publicly rooting for her? Was this some kind of mean prank?

Shrugging it off, she focused on the maneuver. All that mattered now was her routine on the beam. She tried a cartwheel and nailed it, although slowly. Then she squatted low on the beam and extended a leg off to the side and stretched some more, this time as part of the routine she was rehearsing for the meet. The muscles from her feet up to her neck felt strong and tested from the ongoing practices.

She reached back into an arch, the joints in her neck creaking, and held it for ten painful seconds. Like a scorpion she curled her legs forward over her head and placed her feet on the beam. She did a full turn followed by a forward roll and then some more stretches.

When she dismounted, Donna came over. "Hey, you're looking good, Sara."

No Bird's Nest this time? Sara wondered. *Is Donna actually being nice to me? Supportive?*

"Thanks," she said, making eye contact, trying to read Donna's expression. Donna looked sincere so she turned to face the other girls. "That means a lot to me, Donna, and coming from an excellent gymnast like you…"

Coach Jane blew her whistle again and Sara hustled to the next station. Later, when practice was over, she put on her street clothes in the locker room and hurried through the gym toward the exit.

Donna and Zoe were by the door and her hopes of their acceptance grew as they smiled at her.

But those hopes were dashed, when behind the two girls Lauren entered the studio and pulled Donna and Zoe in close.

"Ready for lunch?" Lauren said loudly, her eyes spotting Sara and giving her a stern look. A look that meant, *Stay away from my friends.*

The three girls left to have lunch, and Sara went out to the parking lot to look for her brother's car.

Chapter Sixteen

In the car Josh noticed her dejected look.

"More girl problems?" he said, nudging her elbow. "What happened?"

But she didn't want to share her embarrassment with him. She just shook her head, and at home he let her inside and left her alone. She stopped at the bathroom to wash up and got a glass of water from the kitchen.

Taking a few gulps of the water as she strode back to her bedroom, she entered and placed the glass down on her computer desk. She sat and Plume appeared from nowhere, leaping onto the chair's arm rest. Sara stroked Plume's back, and the kitty arched her spine and warbled with appreciation. Because it was the weekend, Sara didn't have homework. She turned on her computer and clicked to open the internet icon. The computer was old, a hand-me-down from Josh, and the connection was slow. She waited. Plume leapt onto her lap and wedged between her belly and the desk.

"If I were doing my homework I'd kick you out of here, cat," she told her growing kitten. Plume glanced up at the sound of her voice, and stared at her face through half-shut eyes of contentment. A bead of drool clung to the fur on the kitty's chin. "But it's Saturday and I don't have any homework." She stared at her Facebook page. Not a single pointy red flag notification. Not a single human was thinking about her. To her cat, she said, "I didn't want to go to all those phony social chat places anyway." Lifting her poofy tail, Plume shifted on Sara's lap. "Would you like to play?" Sara said, trying to keep the cat's interest.

Plume mewed and jumped down but circled, awaiting Sara.

"Oh my gosh, I love you. At least somebody loves me back."

Sara shut off the computer—her phone, too—and she and Plume played together for a long time with the young cat leaping through the air at the mouse on the string…exhibiting amazing feats of agility.

Chapter Seventeen

The gym at Northern Virginia Community College buzzed with excitement as Sara stepped out onto the floor. She paused to look around. Girls in uniforms surrounded her, leotards of red, white, and blue; white and blue; crimson; maroon; purple; and even orange. No sign yet of the bright-yellow-with-green-trim colors of her school. From the bleachers, cameras flashed as proud parents took photos of their daughters.

She forced herself not to look for her mother in the crowd, though she knew her mother was watching her. Seeing no familiar faces, she headed across the large blue rectangular mat insulating the gymnasium floor. At least she was dressed and on time, having already registered at the front desk where she'd gotten her assigned number 311, and learned that her first event was the balance beam.

The thought of the beam, even chaperoned, gave her a chill. She could fall, like she'd fallen from the unevens. Coach Jane would be there to catch her, just in case, but the uneven bars were an unpredictable thing.

"All right!" came a loud voice.

Sara scanned the crowd on the floor. Girls were trotting toward a young woman in an official judge's uniform. "Time to assemble," the tournament official told them.

Sara looked around, and Kyle's face was the first she recognized. He spotted her and hurried over to pull her into the assembly, placing her behind fellow eleven-year-old Michelle Lee, who also wore the green Phoenix uniform. She knew Michelle from school. She was cool, but didn't talk with Sara much.

Since joining Phoenix, Sara had been dazzled by Michelle's skills.

She's so good, and I—

Team Phoenix stood, shoulder to shoulder, and Coach Jane appealed to their faces, one at a time, and then focused on Sara.

"Michelle and Sara, Squad One, to the beam." Coach Jane's eyes locked onto Sara's. "I'll assist." The coach turned to her assistant coach. "Kyle, take Zoe and Donna to the unevens. Youngsters to the big mat for the floor event." Coach Jane nudged Ryland and Melanie through a break in the stream of passing gymnasts. "I'll be over before you start. Stretch like we practiced."

Music played, some classical march.

"Oh, I almost forgot the little parade first." Sara gathered from Coach Jane's tone that the woman held a low regard for the opening ceremony.

Following the official tournament lady's instructions, the girls were led around the outside of the rectangular mat, the procession being videotaped by hundreds of phone-bearing supporters in the bleachers while the symphony sound played over the PA system.

Kyle caught up to walk alongside of her. *What did he want now?*

Matching her pace, he leaned in and said, "Be good today, Sara."

She kept walking and smiling as she was supposed to. Just ahead of Michelle was Donna, Zoe in front of her. They marched and waved to the crowd, smiling. *Sara felt ridiculous.*

The queue of girls rounded the final corner, Sara a part of it. She followed Michelle, and together they formed the middle of the line of gymnasts, the coaches walking alongside on either side of the procession.

Aside from Kyle being goofy cute, his words carried an inspirational jolt that fired up her blood. She could hear the crowd and did not fear it, instead it fueled her, and she looked out at the equipment and felt familiar with it, as if it were her natural habitat.

"Strength and balance," Kyle added, before moving ahead to pretend as if he were directing the line. "Strength and balance."

The line turned to acknowledge different sections of the auditorium, and the crowd applauded and hooted with anticipation for the meet.

A different song started, some sort of old-fashioned American anthem. Kyle and the other team's coaches led them around again and they were joined by the event commissioner, a woman in her forties who wore the official event commissioner's uniform: a crimson sweat suit, with beige stripes down the sides. Dangling from the commissioner's chest was a golden medallion that would be given to the tournament champion. She took over the leadership of the line, and they all followed her now, waving to the appreciative crowd.

Sara followed and did what she was expected to do, smile and wave toward any members of support in the crowd; in her case, her mother. This time she looked up and searched for her mom's lime green sweater but couldn't find her. The procession stopped and the girls lined up according to their squads. Sara spotted Donna in her green and yellow leotard towering over the other girls in Squad Three.

Coach Jane came over. "At your pace, today, Sara," she said.

She squatted in the middle of the team huddle and rambled out last-minute instructions to each of the girls.

On the chant of "Phoenix!" Donna and Zoe joined gymnasts from Leesburg and Ashburn at the uneven bars event.

A girl from Leesburg, dressed in her school's colors, red and black, started her aerial display. She did okay, a safe routine and she'd landed off-balance on her dismount. When Zoe's turn came, she gave a solid performance, peaking and bringing a few hoots during her twisting double reverse somersault. A freckled-armed redhead from Ashburn went next, and Sara watched until her thoughts turned inward and she watched no more, though her eyes remained on the event.

"Sara!" Coach Jane hollered. "You're up!" Sara swallowed and followed Coach across the gym.

To her left Ryland, Melanie, and two other girls started their practice moves, focusing on their own movements yet respecting the space of others. The walk across the gym gave Sara time to think and she didn't want to think because she knew she'd start doubting herself again. She didn't want to start with the beam—she wanted to be out there on the bare mat now, doing her floor exercise to get the jitters out and get it over with.

"Stick to your planned routine," Coach Jane said over the din of the crowd. "Keep it simple. It's an early step on the path back."

It could be worse, she thought, sitting down to stretch. At least she didn't have to start on the unevens. Those bars, which would always remind her of how close she'd come to death. How she'd tumbled just a little too far around and landed directly on her chest...just inches from having been paralyzed for the rest of her life, or worse.

She faced the crowd and this time picked out Mom in her brilliant lime green sweater. Mom saw her looking and smiled and gave her a fist of encouragement.

Sara nodded and faced the event. A girl from Ashburn had started her routine, but with Donna heading toward the bars she didn't want to miss her teammate's performance. She was sure Lauren Brimes was in the crowd somewhere watching, as well, cheering on Donna and Zoe.

And hoping to see me fall. Despite her mom's fist of encouragement, she didn't want to go on. She felt faint.

Coach Jane leaned down to get her attention. "You're up right after Michelle. She's next."

Sara's attention returned to the balance beam. The blonde on it now was a short and stocky girl from

Lovettsville, doing one twisting somersault after another just as a warm-up.

How can I possibly compete against that? she wondered. *I'll be lucky if I don't fall and break my neck.* Her last thought brought a shiver.

Not knowing any of the other girls there, she sat down cross-legged, closed her eyes and blocked out the noises inside the gym and began to imagine herself performing her balance beam routine to perfection.

But instead it was like having a nightmare all over again...the overcompensation during her dismount, the crushing collision with the mat, the blackness, and then the excruciating waking pain. She tried to push the vision from her mind and focus on something positive that would get her through her routine... What was it again?

"Come on," Coach Jane said, helping her to her feet. "I'll be right there."

Coach Jane turned to watch Michelle, who was now owning the beam as if it were an extension of her body, finding each step, whether looking or not, turning on her toes, cartwheeling, somersaulting and dismounting to perfection.

"Balance, confidence, and strength," Coach said, just as Kyle had.

Michelle dismounted with a flurry of aerial maneuvers landing perfectly on her feet. Coach Jane and others hooted and clapped.

Oh, no.

The moment she had dreaded was here, her return to the pressures, and as she had learned earlier in life, the dangers of competition. Coach would be helping her this first time out, but she needed more than that to approach the beam.

A vision of Plume leapt across her mind's eye, the young cat's playful agility.

Sara placed both hands on the beam and, using her arms, pushed her feet off the mat. She extended her right leg up and over into a straddling position and then lifted her feet and placed her toes behind her on the beam. Pushing with her arms, her knees came up touching the beam just for a moment and then she was on her feet. She raised her arms and smiled at the thought of her kitty and launched into a cartwheel to ignite her routine. With a quick turn, she did a forward roll back, a back walkover. Coach Jane shuffled alongside the beam, trying to keep up.

When the judges awarded her score, she shut her eyes and thanked God for getting her through the event, the first time she'd competed in two years. Her score wasn't too bad, either: a seven!

She earned a near-perfect score on the floor, second only to a near-perfect Michelle, who had executed a series of handsprings and then gone back the other way, leaving many in the audience open-mouthed. Sticking to her own plan, her own current abilities, Sara kept her floor routine simple and she performed it without error.

Following a couple of decent vault scores, she headed into the final event well-lathered and confident. But when her eyes landed on the uneven bars, her chest heaved, her belly slumped and her legs teetered. Her breath short, her heart pounding from anxiety, she spun toward the exit and trotted away.

If any of the other Phoenix girls or coaches noticed her, they didn't say anything. There were no shouts after her as she escaped into the lady's locker room. The door closed behind her and shut out the noise from the arena.

They probably think I'm rushing to the toilet, she thought, and in her uncomfortable state the notion wasn't far from the truth.

She found the empty bench and sat. Letting out a squeak, she slid to her left, into the locker-room shadows. Her head fell into her hands, her scraggly dark hair escaping the bun her mother had put it in, and she cried.

The door to the locker room opened, letting in light and noise. A tentative male voice said, "Sara?"

Oh my gosh... Kyle. He must have seen me leave the gym. She sniffed away the tears but new ones pooled in her eyes. "Yeah?" she called, her voice cracking.

"You okay?"

She gazed toward the open door, but it was obscured by the row of lockers. "Yeah."

"You ran off," Kyle continued from the doorway. "I was concerned."

"I'll be right out," she said, though she wasn't certain that would be the truth. She glanced up at her designated locker, debating whether she should put her street clothes over her uniform and run home. Run away.

Kyle was silent for a moment, then said, "Hold on, I'm sending Michelle in."

In a panic, Sara stood and tried the combination on her locker. Once she had it open, she grabbed her spare towel and wiped the tears and snot from her face.

Michelle's voice came from behind her, "Hey, girl."

Sara took her time turning. "Yeah?"

"You okay?" Michelle cocked her head into the shadowy part of the locker to study Sara's face.

"Yes," Sara said, her tone impatient this time.

"I thought you were going to watch me on the unevens. Something must be wrong."

Sara frowned. It wasn't Michelle's fault. With a nod, she said, "Yeah, I'm sorry. I just didn't feel good for a moment there. I'll be right back out."

She placed her towel back in the locker and when she faced forward Michelle was still there.

"I know what happened to you..." Michelle said, "...two years ago?"

Sara waited.

Michelle rounded the bench and stood next to Sara. She put her hand on Sara's shoulder. "We're all rooting for you out there today. Come on."

Sara shuddered at the thought of going back out there now. With all the people who must have seen her run into the locker room like a frightened rabbit. "Nuh-no," she stammered.

Insistent, Michelle took her hand and pulled. Sara followed and Kyle was just outside the door, her safety net before facing the crowd of other gymnasts, judges, coaches, parents, and kids who might notice her.

"All right, Sara," Kyle said as Michelle returned to watch the competition. "Time for a pep talk."

She swallowed and checked the floor behind Kyle, and then the bleachers. No one seemed to be paying attention to her, which was good.

He said, "We all have something we think about that makes us feel good, no matter where we are or what we're doing, right?"

Avoiding his gaze, she nodded politely then sniffled.

"And when we think about this one thing it relaxes us, no matter how sad or nervous or angry we are, right?"

Again she nodded and then heard Michelle's name called for the uneven bars. Michelle had risked missing her turn to fetch her out of the locker room.

Maybe other people do care about me...

"What makes you smile, Sara? What makes you smile so naturally that you don't even know you're smiling?" Kyle asked.

"Nothing," she whispered.

"What?"

"Nothing."

"I don't believe that for a second. Think harder."

Kyle's crazy yet confident eyes remained on her face, like a persistent friend trying to help her despite her refusal. She thought and in her mind she saw Plume again.

"There it is," Kyle said with a chuckle. "That smile of yours that sneaks out every once in a while. What are you thinking about?"

She heard the applause for Michelle and felt bad Kyle was wasting time with her when other students were competing. She'd have to answer to try to get Kyle's attention back to Michelle and the others.

"My kitty, Plume."

Kyle nodded and then gestured toward her next station. "When you're up on the bars, don't think about the judges or the crowd or the other contestants. Think about your kitty, Plume. What does she teach you?"

Sara didn't answer but she approached the bars, knowing the answer.

"Confidence," he called to her.

With a jerk of her head, Coach Jane prompted her, and Sara leapt up and hung from the lower bar. She swung, gathering momentum, and Coach Jane guided her as she jackknifed into a perched position. Not wanting to totally take it slow, she dared the high bar, got it in her grasp and then jackknifed again, her thighs connecting with the bottom of the high bar. She swung her lower body again, another attempt at mounting the high bar...

I can't do it.

Then Kyle's voice surprised her. He seemed to be everywhere... shouldn't he be coaching somewhere?

"Your kitty, Plume," Kyle said.

The unevens posed the risk of a bad fall, but when she thought of Plume and the cat's quiet confidence and daring, Sara loosened some key parts of her body, and twirled on the bar. Her stomach took a split second of force, and then her limbs took over her hips, and she planted her feet on the bar, and pretended she was a cat. Crazy like a cat. Unafraid of falling. Or failing.

She thought of all the times Plume had landed slightly off balance but on her paws nonetheless, and smiled and continued her routine. She didn't have the strength yet but she had the courage now, and the balance...

"Take it easy, Sara," Coach Jane said, supporting her. "I've got you."

Sara twirled on the upper bar, and launched into her dismount. The flipping maneuver felt a little wrong, her left hip going out of alignment, her legs hooking left. Coach Jane was there, cradling her and righting her. She placed her feet and after a stutter-step, stopped on the mat, and raised her arms.

She heard a *woot* from the crowd, then polite clapping.

Despite her nerves and overall anxiety, she'd performed okay. She'd gotten back up on the bars, and that was a huge step. A step she never imagined she'd be able to take again.

Sara trotted off the mat toward where Coach Jane and the rest of the Phoenix team waited. Donna was the first to congratulate her. "You did great, girl. Very nice for your first time back."

"That's right," Coach Jane said. "And pretty good for a first step back if you ask me."

The final gymnast on the bars took her turn. They would have to be relatively quiet now, but still Coach Jane threw her arm around Sara's shoulders and gave her a supportive hug.

Chapter Eighteen

Sara's mom opened the front door and the two of them went inside. Josh had scribbled a note in plain view on the kitchen counter saying he was out with a friend.

A friend, Sara thought dolefully. *I wonder what that's like.* After the meet, once again Donna and Zoe had left with Lauren Brimes while Sara had gone home with her mommy. She moped toward her room.

"Hey," Mom called as Sara reached the hall. Sara turned sluggishly. Her mother approached and took her by the wrist. "Sara, I want you to listen to me. You did great," she said, slowly emphasizing the last three words.

Sara nodded. Mom was right, at least in terms of two of the events. She'd finished second out of eight girls in the floor exercise and fifth on the balance beam out of nine contestants. The vault and bars, where she'd finished last, were a different story, however. Coming in dead last frustrated her, making her wish for the days before her fall, when she used to win these events. But all things considered, she was pleased with how she had gone out and competed today. Sara was smart enough to know she couldn't just take top honors virtually overnight.

But still in life over all, she was not doing great. She hadn't a friend in the world, and she felt lonely and foolish everywhere she went. She hurried to her bedroom.

While lying face down on the mattress, her head hanging over the side, she saw something poke out from beneath the bed. A small, white paw with a dark brown splotch on the toe. "Oh, Plume, you little peeper." With a giggle, Sara leaned over the side of the bed and dragged her fingers across the carpet. Plume swiped at her hand, her soft pads and the tufts of white fur tickling her. Then the cat's head appeared, and Plume squirmed and bit Sara's thumb.

"Ouch! Ha-ha." Sara seized Plume and, despite the feline's jerking motions to free herself, brought the pet up to the bed. On the mattress, she stroked Plume from head to tail, and Plume nudged her with her furry head and bared her teeth in play.

Despite Plume's pleasant distraction, Sara's thoughts returned to the envy she'd felt when the short and stocky blonde girl from Lovettsville had stood on the gold platform to receive her top honors earlier today—only a certificate, a piece of paper was all it was really, but a piece of paper Sara desired. She knew if she could be good at something again she'd get some respect...and she remembered the other two top girls at today's tournament, Michelle and Donna, from her own school, obtaining second and third best for the day. She could have been that good if only —

With her fingernails, Sara combed Plume's sideburns. "You're not afraid of getting hurt, are you, little Princess Plume?"

Plume's snout and cheek rubbed Sara's wrist.

"Your whiskers tickle. I wish I had time to play with you, but I'm going to a basketball game with Josh tonight. You know, riding along?" She picked her cat up and kissed her on her furry forehead. "It's kind of sad how much you mean to me, little kitty. What did Mr. Hamid call you? A Turkish Van Cat?"

A knock on her door.

"Sara!" Josh's voice called from outside in the hall. "We're leaving now." He knocked again and said, "We don't want to miss the tipoff."

"Coming!" she called.

He rapped the door again. "Okay, but hurry up. We want to get good seats."

Sara put Plume down and grabbed her only decent pair of jeans from the dresser and pulled them over her leotard. She forced her leg down the pant leg then followed with the other leg. Then, standing up, she pulled.

Time short, she nonetheless continued her conversation with her kitty as she finished dressing. "I'll be home late. Keep the bed warm for us, Princess Plume."

She kissed Plume on the forehead, quickly, so the wild kitty wouldn't swat at her and joined her brother by the front door.

Josh drove them to the game in silence and the mid-February night made the seven p.m. roads dark and the surrounding woodlands sinister. Sara wondered if going to a gymnasium full of crowded people, most of whom she didn't know, was a good idea. On the floorboards and on the beam it had been different. Nobody close to hinder her movements, her expression, her attempt to be good at something. It was just her and the mats and the beam.

A trio of clumsy boys bumped into her as she followed her brother toward the gate. People were everywhere, darting in all directions, cutting her off and making it difficult to keep up with Josh.

Finally, he stopped and she got behind him in one of several lines leading inside the arena. They bought their tickets and entered a nearly packed arena. The basketball players were all standing and receiving last minute instructions from the coach. She peered into the crowd, and after some searching spotted a few familiar faces. Someone waved to her as she and Josh climbed toward a couple of empty bleachers seats. Sara's eyes locked onto the person... It was Donna, towering over Zoe, and Lauren on her other side, silently glaring at her from the noisy crowd. She lifted her hand briefly to wave back to Donna, and then went to sit with her brother.

Before she reached the seat, a boy in a Jefferson High School jacket scooted into the last space in the row, right next to Josh. Josh looked at her and shrugged. She spotted another spot on a bench two rows up and continued to climb the bustling aisle.

Got to be fearless, she told herself as she took her seat alone, two rows above Josh, and a few rows beneath where the hateful Lauren sat with Donna and Zoe. Quickly the arena's remaining seats were taken and the tension of a rivalry game filled the air, the murmur of the crowd, the hustling, squeaking sounds from rubber-soled sneakers scraping the court below, and then abruptly the scoreboard blared and the noise stopped. Sara gazed around as the players headed back to their benches one last time before tipoff.

The overhead scoreboard reset to the start of the first quarter, with Visitor 0, Home 0. Sara and Josh below had pretty good seats. They were about halfway up the stands, twenty feet above and directly in back of the Percyville team bench. The guys from her town were wearing home white tank tops and white boxer shorts, with green trim. To their left the other team, Jefferson High School, wore the visiting maroon with yellow trim. Across the gym behind the visiting team's bench, the crowd was largely decked out in maroon and yellow.

A whistle blew and the ref threw the ball in the air at midcourt. Tommy Schmidt leapt and swatted it back to his teammate, Andy Lee, Michelle's older brother who played point guard for Percyville High. The home crowd applauded, and Andy dribbled the ball toward the defense and passed the ball out to another Percyville player who lobbed it into tall Tommy who tapped his shot off the backboard and in. The home fans roared, but the visiting team from Jefferson, the Bobcats as they were called, glided down the court quickly and sank a shot from far away.

At times the Bobcats made the local kids from Percyville look slow, and even the quick Andy Lee looked suddenly sullen and exhausted. Near the end of the first half, the Jefferson team held a 24 to 17 lead, had the ball, and appeared to be in control of the game. The tallest kid on Jefferson caught a pass under the basket and when the Percyville defense surrounded him, he threw it back outside to a swift moving guard who faced the basket and shot. The ball swished through the netted basket on the buzzer, a three-pointer, and Sara glanced up at the scoreboard: 27 to 17 at halftime.

This side of the gymnasium moaned.

"Hey," a voice said and Sara felt someone grabbing her wrist. She turned and saw that Donna had climbed down the bleachers to say hello. "Gimme five," Donna said. Sara stared at Donna's proffered hand for a second and then slapped the girl's palm with her own. Donna said, "Some game, huh? Is this your first?"

"Yep," Sara said, subconsciously glancing up at Zoe and Lauren. Lauren watched with a scornful expression. "I like it, but I hope our boys take over in the second half."

No sooner was she wondering why Donna had come down at the halftime whistle, when Zoe, too, stepped down, leaving Lauren temporarily alone. Was this sudden show of support because she was part of the gymnastics team now, and Lauren wasn't? Had Donna and Zoe suddenly tired of Lauren's insulting ways? Lauren was still popular, but aside from junior-high cheerleading and being pretty and popular, was she really liked?

As if sensing Sara's scrutiny of her, Lauren stepped down over the seats vacated by fans going for refreshments or to the bathrooms. Lauren hopped down next to Donna, the scowl on her face telling them she was not happy, and said, "What's going on?"

Without looking at Lauren, Donna said, "I came down to talk about the game with Sara... Sara, whaddya think of the game so far?"

Appreciating Donna's courage to defy Lauren, Sara smiled. "I'm enjoying it... I wish Percyville was winning, though." She brushed a tangle of hair out of her eyes, looked down and waited.

Zoe interrupted the silence, surprising them all with her sudden social outburst. "Great idea, Donna. I think we should sit with Sara."

"Yeah! It's closer to the action!" Lauren Brimes blurted. She laughed and slapped Zoe's arm. "Zoe told me she had a crush on Kyle and she wants to be as close to the bench as possible."

Zoe flushed and quietly said, "You weren't supposed to tell any—"

"I'll sit next to Sara," Donna interrupted and sat next to Sara as if she were the girl's best friend in the whole world. Sara and Donna's eyes met, and Sara smiled gratefully. *Things are getting better.*

The second half started and Andy Lee dribbled the ball up for Percyville. He looked rested now and he accelerated around a Jefferson player and dished the ball out to Patrick Haskin who fired up a shot and missed. The ball bounced high and a Jefferson kid got the rebound and raced down court. The rebounder delivered a perfect bounce pass to the tall kid who leapt from the floor and dunked the basketball.

Most of the crowd moaned again, and then Donna said, "Our boys need some kind of spark. Maybe Zoe can strut down there and kiss Kyle on the lips."

They all laughed at this one and the uncomfortable game went on...on the court and in the bleachers, and all but Lauren played. Even Sara, who had every reason to hate Lauren, felt sorry for the way Donna and Zoe had turned on their former group leader.

"Oh, no," Donna said, grasping her head as another demoralizing slam dunk hushed the home crowd and put Jefferson up by the score of 35-21. The Percyville coaches called a timeout and in the brooding quiet of the crowd Lauren Brimes said, "Hey, Bird's Nest, what's the idea coming to the game tonight and intruding on me and my friends?"

The slur of *Bird's Nest* stunned her, its ugliness on yet another girl's lips, this time Lauren's. Had Lauren invented the term? Had Donna only overheard it and repeated it like a parrot?

Sara wheeled to face the bully, her nostrils flaring, her teeth bared. But she did not strike, though she felt she had a right to. No, that was not what she was, and so she offered little resistance as Lauren grabbed her and surprisingly quickly lifted her off the seat and into the air. Lauren Brimes's lips puckered in sadistic delight as she shoved Sara down toward the court.

In self-defense, Sara cocked her neck and placed a hand on a man's back, then after a cartwheeling motion, her foot pushed off the bleacher seat and she continued to flip and tumble, so far safely, toward the hardwood floor.

A whistle blew as one of the referees noticed the commotion in the stands, and Sara saw the shiny floor of the basketball court nearing her face. She thought of Plume, and then she *"let it rip"* as Donna had once urged, and with a quiet grunt of execution she performed a perfect pirouetting somersault and landed on her feet. She raised her arms and looked around. The game had stopped. Everyone was looking at her.

"But it wasn't my fault," she said.

And then someone starting clapping, and others joined in, and Kyle came over, his eyes showing concern. "Are you all right?"

Before she could utter a reply, Kyle jerked his head in the direction of the bleachers. Sara glanced to see who he might be glaring at and caught a glimpse of Lauren making her way up the rafters, trying to get away. Many of the spectators shouted at her, asking her why she would push another girl out of the bleachers.

"You could have broken her neck!" a man hollered.

Sara didn't see any security guards following Lauren as she strode out into the lobby. Next to her, Kyle remained, his presence warming her.

In a daze, she looked at him. The game was still at a halt. It was silent and she felt everyone's eyes upon her and Kyle.

"Can I escort you back to your seat, Sara?" Kyle said.

He walked her all the way up and back to her seat, and with just Donna and Zoe seated beside her now, Sara breathed deeply and easily, realizing she had just escaped a near-death experience. And as she relaxed and tried to come back to normal sensations, the Percyville team came alive. Tommy Schmidt nailed a three-point shot and the crowd made some noise for the first time in a long time, and following a steal and pass from Andy Lee, Tommy did his own spectacular slam dunk. On the wall of the gym, the electronic scoreboard registered the now-close score: 38 to 33 in favor of the visiting Jefferson team.

Donna patted Sara on the elbow and said, "Hey, I think you ignited the team with your airborne recovery story."

Zoe laughed as Sara smiled and the boys from Percyville began fighting their way back. She occasionally glanced down at Kyle near the home bench, and she noticed a shift in body language and momentum. Assistant Coach Kyle barked at the players and some of them even barked back. This was their game now.

Elated from Donna and Zoe's companionship and the thrill of the Percyville Eagles' sensational performance, Sara cheered when the buzzer sounded and the boys from Percyville celebrated a 51 to 48 victory at midcourt.

What a comeback!

And as if to confirm her suspicions that things were getting better, Kyle looked up and found her in the crowd and smiled at her.

Chapter Nineteen

Josh bombarded her with questions the entire car ride back from the game. How had she done that? Landed on her feet? And why had Lauren shoved her?

The night sky was dark but when they reached their home street, the street lamps and neighboring porch lights shone brightly enough to illuminate a black limousine idling by the curb. Josh's car passed the long limo as he parked at the bottom of their short driveway. The front light was on and Sara scrambled out of the passenger seat with the feeling of dread building in the pit of her stomach. She looked through the front window to see her mother and a man seated inside. "All right, what's going on?" she said.

Ignoring her question, Josh let them into the kitchen. "I mean, was all that gymnastics stuff planned, Sear Bear? Did you practice that move just to show off at the game tonight?" He glanced around the kitchen. "Mom?"

Sara headed toward the living room where she heard soft, cautious voices.

Josh called to her, "I mean, the whole thing was a publicity stunt, right? Lauren is in on it, and she pushed you and you knew it was coming and... I don't believe what I saw—"

They rounded the corner, and in the den with Mom sat the almost forgotten Orkhan Hamid, the man who claimed to be a descendant of Turkish Sultans, wearing his tall hat and long facial hair. His head swiveled in Sara's direction, and the intensity of his gaze with his dark and penetrating eyes made her pause. Then something else on the man's face drew her attention, and she lifted her gaze. Below Mr. Hamid's headdress the beauty mark revealed itself. Strangely, she could see it up close now. Thick black hairs grew from this mole on his forehead, and the mutating mass of skin changed from brown to orange before Sara's eyes.

Mr. Hamid studied Mom's tea cup and snickered before taking a sip of tea. The two adults sat casually as if sharing a secret and Sara thought the worst.

"Mom, please tell me you didn't?"

Mom and Mr. Hamid both looked up, and then Orkhan Hamid slapped his knee and laughed.

"Please join us, young Sara." Mr. Hamid nodded and gestured toward the sofa where he sat; Mom faced him from the chair. "I was just explaining to your mother again how much this breed of cat and my family have been through together. One time there came a terrible earthquake in 1976, and my aging great uncle Abdul Orkhan Hamid the Fourth, who, like me, would have been a true heir to the throne that was no longer honored by the people, got trapped under the rubble of his decaying palace. His special cat, Azreal, was a crafty animal and totally loyal to my uncle. This cat squeezed its way down into the rubble where Uncle Abdul was trapped and licked his nose with its gritty tongue and then led rescuers to the great sultan in waiting."

Mr. Hamid trailed off wistfully. He wiped a tear from his cheek as he continued. He gazed into Sara's eyes and she couldn't look away. Her mind drifting...

"Another time back in the fifteenth century, the great Sultan Murad was saved from drowning in the royal bath when his prized cat, Uda, dove into the pool and roused him by biting his nose."

"Uh, Mr. Hamid," Sara's mom interrupted, instantly bringing Sara out of her trance. She heard her mom say, "This is all very touching, but my answer is still no."

Josh who'd been silent finally uttered what had been running through his mind. "Mom, this guy is a fake. Mr. Hamid, we'd like you to leave."

"Josh!" Mom snapped. "Mr. Hamid, I apologize for my son's rudeness. I am sympathetic to how much this cat's bloodline may be related to your family's history, but the cat is legally ours." She gave Sara an assuring glance. "And we will not sell this cat to you at any price."

You tell him, Mom! Plume was hers and would be hers until either she or the cat died...and even then. Where was she, by the way? Sara glanced around, avoiding Mr. Hamid's penetrating gaze. Excusing herself from the den, she went to look for her cat.

Plume lay on the bed, waiting. Sara nestled down beside the cat and stroked her head and then face. Plume mewed.

She heard the goodbyes and the sound of the front door shutting as Mr. Hamid left. Plume hissed. It was a mournful little squeak, as if both Sara and her kitty knew they hadn't seen the last of Orkhan Hamid.

Chapter Twenty

The hard practices had bonded them as a unit, and all the work, sweat, and time created camaraderie among the girls. The other girls stretched with Sara, talked to her when they needed to, and when the school year ended, Michelle even sent Sara an invitation for her birthday pool party. Sara accepted and Mom had given her consent.

On Saturday at noon, the team, once again, relaxed together around Michelle's pool and patio with its sculpted garden and blooming plants, the lounge chairs, the crystal clear, refreshing pool. No cake and ceremony this time. Just girls having fun. Sara sat in one of the chairs and let the sun beat down on her head and shoulders as she basked in its warmth with the tingling of pleasure coursing up her spine. Her thoughts were on the swimming pool just below her feet, she no longer felt the chill of Orkhan Hamid's hypnotic stare or the cruelness of Lauren Grimes's actions. It was summertime, and those things that had previously plagued her during the school year were now a distant memory. Amid shrill laughter, a beach ball rolled across the patio toward her. She reached forward from her chair and tapped it toward Michelle who took it, spun and spiked it at Donna. For most of the school year, she hadn't even realized Michelle lived in the house right behind her own. Now that she had friends she knew a lot of things. She'd met Michelle's brother, Andy, the basketball player, on previous visits, and had been invited over to Donna's and even Zoe's homes on a couple of occasions. Lauren Brimes, no longer a hostile distraction, was attending summer school and hitting the books to avoid further discipline from the school and her parents. Sara had even taken alternative champion honors in the Fairfax County Gymnastics Tournament. Things were definitely better.

No, she corrected herself. *Things are great.*

Her skin was getting hot so she got out of the chair where she'd been sunning and pulled her hair back into a ponytail. She padded over to the shade of a shrub at the edge of the patio where her security blanket, Plume, lay tied to the fence with a small bowl of water placed nearby. She was an outdoor cat now, to an extent. When the school year ended, Sara bought her a collar and leash and began taking her for short walks with each walk getting farther. Before long, Plume seemed to know her way around the neighborhood, leading Sara during their walks.

"I'm just going for a quick dip," she told the cat and bent down to rub Plume's face. "Your water's right there if you get thirsty." Sara trotted across the hot stone patio and leapt into the low end of the pool, splashing Michelle. How amazing was it that Michelle lived practically next door, just a short hike down the wooded path? Now she had a friend with a pool. Life was really good, and Sara breathed in a cool breath of contentment.

Life was great.

"Sara, we need one more person for volleyball," Zoe called to her from the pool. "You're on my team."

They played, imagining a net raised between them. Donna and Michelle spiked the ball down on the two shorter girls. Sara made an occasional diving save, tapping the ball to Zoe, and they had cool, refreshing, splashing summer fun.

"Wait, what's that?" Michelle shrieked. Sara whirled in time to see Plume, free of her leash, scurry to the coping on the opposite side of the pool. Sara swam toward the cat, amazed not only that Plume had gotten loose but that she had chosen to join them by the pool and not run away. She accidentally swallowed water, but kept swimming.

If I ever lose that cat, my luck's over, Sara thought. She placed a hand on the coping next to Plume, and the cat sniffed Sara's watery hand and let Sara pet her. *I'm starting to sound like Mr. Hamid, with all his superstitions about you.*

Plume cocked her head and then lowered her white paw with the brown toe and tested the water of the pool.

"Ha! Your cat likes water." Michelle swam over and stood next to Sara in the low end. They were soon joined by Donna and Zoe.

"Well, so much for our game," Donna said. "Maybe you do have a special kind of cat, Sara, unlike what Lauren was spewing on about. Does it swim?"

Sara glanced back at Donna and smiled. "It's a she and I don't know." She turned back to her cat and the answer to Donna's question came in a sudden blur of motion... Plume leapt from the coping and, with a soft splash, landed to Sara's left.

Plume's long coat floated while she beat her paws and kept her face above water. Her plush, feather-like tail dragged behind her, like a beaver's.

"Ha-ha-ha," Michelle blurted. They all pointed and laughed and Sara laughed so hard she couldn't breathe. Finally, she caught her breath and paddled after her cat, but the cat angled right, toward the cement steps leading out of Michelle's pool. Plume emerged from the water and trotted up the final shallow step and then shook herself off, sprinkling the patio. Sara strode up after the cat and squatted beside Plume who was now licking herself dry with her sandpaper tongue that Sara had so many times felt on her hands, feet, and face.

"That was the funniest thing I have ever seen in my life, Princess," Sara said with a giggle. "Were you cooling off?" And then including the other girls, she said more loudly, "Do you think you can do that for us again?"

Plume twisted her face in a look of contempt and then raised her tail as she turned and headed toward the shade of the hedges.

Chapter Twenty-One

The best thing about being a kid in summer was you could do whatever you felt like doing and Michelle had them all back to her pool after practice the next day—all except the fiercely independent Plume. Sara felt it wise to keep Plume at home this time, so she couldn't get loose. Who knew where she might trot off to the next time, given the chance?

They swam and sunbathed and talked for hours. At five, Sara said her goodbyes to everyone and hugged Michelle on the way out. She walked home in her flip flops using the path through the woods.

Smelling of chlorine, her hair still wet, she opened the back door to her house and went inside. Lincoln greeted her by the back porch, a guilty and timid look in his eyes.

"What did you do, old boy?" she said, sniffing. She headed up the hall toward the kitchen, her eyes searching the floors. There wasn't a bad smell so she went to her room to check on Plume. Plume wasn't on the bed, or under it. She wasn't in the closet or in the corners of the room, or under the dresser, where she could no longer fit anyway.

"Plume?" Sara called as she stepped back out into the hall. She strode toward the rear of the house. "Here, kitty, kitty, kitty." Turning back to the kitchen, she removed a large sealed pouch with a cartoon drawing of a happy cat on the label. "Want a treat?" Sara called. "Plume?"

The cat did not appear by walking across the kitchen floor or jumping up onto a counter top which she did when she was being naughty. Her concern growing, Sara searched the entire house, every closet, under every bed... She ran to the window, then to the next, then to the back door. Nothing was open, no way for the cat to have gotten out... Or was there?

In a daze she wandered near the back door and picked her phone out of her duffle bag where she'd left it. She pressed her mom's number and waited. When her mom didn't answer on her own cell phone, she tried the coffee shop number, and waited again. "Why won't you pick up—?" Finally, her mom's voice said hello.

"Mom, I came home from Michelle's pool party and can't find Plume."

"Huh," her mom breathed. "Hold on just a sec, Sara... Um, be right with you." From her mother's tone and the background noise, Sara could tell that the coffee shop was busy, but this was important.

"Mom, I need help," she cried.

"What happened? Is your brother home yet?"

"No. I'm all alone and Plume's missing, Mom!" Sara's heart raced as her mind ran through the possibilities. *Someone accidentally let her outside...or she's still hiding in the house somewhere...or...* She was tired and still dazed from the sun and couldn't think of any other possibility until a shiver started in her chest; it rose up to her throat forcing her to utter the word with an icy gargle. "Hamid."

"What?" her mom said.

"Hamid. I think Orkhan Hamid kidnapped Plume."

"What?" Mom said as if suddenly starting to listen. "Are there any signs of a break-in? Get out of the house until your brother—"

"No, Mom. I checked." She paused to catch her breath, the sinking feeling increasing. "There's no one here but me and Lincoln. Plume always meows or comes out when I call her. I even shook her bag of treats. She's not here."

Through the phone line, Sara's mom exhaled. "Okay, look, I'll call Maggie and have her take over here. I can be home in an hour. Have Josh help you look one more time, and then we'll talk about what to do next."

"But shouldn't we call the police?"

"No." Mom's voice was loud now. "Don't call anyone until we figure out what happened. Bye." Mom hung up.

Sara ended the connection and staggered toward her room. She collapsed onto her bed and cried. Just when everything was starting to go well, her most beloved friend...vanished into thin air, snatched by some sort of diabolical and supernatural force.

Hamid.

No he wasn't an evil wizard, but there had been something about him. Something crazy in his eyes. Did he really think a cat could make the difference in a man's fortune and happiness? Plume had made a difference in hers so she believed there could possibly be some truth to Mr. Hamid's Turkish Van Cat story. And now with Plume gone, Sara felt her recently recovered world coming apart.

Chapter Twenty-Two

"You see here where the frame is dented," Josh said, holding the white aluminum window frame at an angle for Sara to see.

Shaking, on the verge of hysterics, she glanced at the bottom of the frame. Near her brother's thumb, the metal bent inward. She saw a slight crack in the white paint, a strip of silver aluminum beneath.

"Pretty sneaky," Josh said. "They just wedged it a bit while trying to get in and put it back as if nothing had happened." He looked at her. "I'm convinced you're right, Sara. That Turkish clown broke in here and took your cat."

"We have to call Mom," she said, hearing the growing panic in her own voice. "Make her hurry. We've got to find Plume before Mr. Hamid leaves the country with her!"

"Sara, you need to calm down. We'll get her back." Her brother pulled out his cell phone to call and see if their mother was on her way home yet.

"Oh, thank you, Josh," she said as her usually uncaring brother waited for their mother to answer. He appeared cocky the way he stood with the tiny blue phone pressed to his ear, his other hand on his hip, and his hip leaning against the kitchen counter. "Mom...? Mom?" He waited and Sara heard her mother's voice, distant and tinny.

"No, we're all right," Josh said. "It's just that our house got broken into. The only thing missing is Plume."

Josh disconnected the call.

"What did she say?" Sara asked. "Is she coming?"

Slipping his mobile into his jeans pocket, Josh nodded. "She said to stay calm, she's not waiting for Maggie. She's closing up the shop now."

Mom raced home and when she came in the door Sara and Josh took turns convincing their mother that Orkhan Hamid or someone working for him had broken into the house and taken Plume.

"It's the only thing that makes sense," Josh said. "Nothing in the house has been messed with except the window, and the cat that phony wanted so badly is gone."

"What should we do?" Mom asked with a frightened, worried expression.

Sara went over and put her arm around her mother. "We should call the police." She gave Mom a squeeze, showing her appreciation but also to help her make her next point. "And we have to go to the airport right now."

"What?" Her mother gently broke loose.

"Hm." Crinkled lines appeared on Josh's forehead. "The airport?" He looked at her. "You think Hamid will be there?"

Sara shut her eyes and saw her cat in her mind, shrouded in darkness, and through perforations in Plume's shadowy prison, she saw figures moving by, interrupting the rays of light that entered the crate. She heard the sound of hurrying footsteps and voices; commotion. "Yes." She nodded. "I don't have time now to explain how I know...I just know it. We have to go there now!"

Mom refused to drive over the speed limit as Sara and Josh watched black SUVs and limousines, a few with diplomatic license plates, race past them to both sides. By the time they'd parked and found their way to the Turkish Airways check-in desk, it was eight o'clock. Mr. Hamid had had two hours at least to get out of the country with her cat, and she knew he was intelligent enough not to stick around for a possible police investigation into a pet-napping. He would either be flying into Ankara or somewhere near Lake Van.

The only way to find out was... She gulped. "Mom?"

"What do we do now?"

"Mom, you have to buy us tickets. I know he's in there. I know my baby's in there with him."

They all stared beyond the check-in desks toward the bustle of passengers heading in opposite directions, but mostly to their left, toward security and then to the shuttles that would take them to their respective gates.

Mom huffed. "You want me to buy a ticket just to check if Mr. Hamid is by the gate with your cat? Sara, we don't have the money for that kind of longshot, hon."

Sara spun toward her brother, who had helped her argue her points with Mom earlier and had a few great points of his own, but Josh wasn't there. She glanced around. Through the human traffic, she spotted him at the service counter speaking with the young man working there. The man was laughing already. What was Josh saying? The man nodded and patted Josh's hand, and Josh returned with that smug cool-guy look on his face. "Mom, Sara," he said. "Get out the family credit card. If we buy tickets, we can get almost all of our money back."

Mom stammered. "What did you say to him?"

"I asked him about the return policy, and he said as long as we get past security he doesn't see a problem with us going in and out to see off our dear Uncle Orkhan Hamid."

"You told him that?" Sara blurted out. "And he believed you?" But she was too anxious to wait for Josh's reply. "Who am I kidding?" she confessed. "I'm not even sure Mr. Hamid would have taken this airline..." and she was about to give up again when Josh took her by the arm and led her to the ticket desk. "I know what flight he's on." he whispered into her ear. "That nice attendant back there told me."

They waited their turn at security, with Josh stripping off his belt and Mom shaking her head in silence behind them. "How'd you charm that guy back there?" Sara asked her brother.

Josh said, "Hey, the guy said you were cute. He said it was cute how you wanted to say goodbye to your uncle and his cat."

She shoved him playfully and he laughed. "You are such a liar," she said with a grin. "I think drama class is turning you into a natural born liar."

Equipped with three passes aboard Flight 1747 to Ankara, they made their way quickly through security—quickly in the sense that the line was short and they didn't have a lot of carry-ons to be scanned and searched—and then onto the tram, which took them to the gate.

Gate 50 sat halfway down a corridor of other gates, and Sara began cutting through the queues and seating areas. She bumped into a short and skinny businessman as he was preparing to drink his coffee and splashed his face. She saw the end of the corridor, a No Exit sign, and spun and headed back the other way, not concerned if Josh and Mom were following her at this point. And then the sadness hit her, and she choked and sobbed, warm tears streaming down her face. It was hopeless, it was over. She'd lost. Lost her cat and lost.

Then, amid the crowd she noticed the tall hat. Made of linens, it resembled a turban held together by strips of cloth. A bed of padding sat on the very top of the hat, adorned with some kind of symbolic protuberance, and the hat and all its appendages all together stood at least a foot and a half above its wearer's head, making Mr. Hamid stand out from the rest of the passengers.

With no sign of Plume or any containers near Mr. Hamid, she checked for her mom, but couldn't see her through the constant obstruction of the passing throng. Across the aisle, people at Gate 52 started boarding their flight to Paris.

Mr. Hamid would surely have a kitty crate, wouldn't he?

She spun back and to her instant panic she no longer saw the top of Mr. Hamid's hat in the area it had been before. Unable to find him as her eyes panned the terminal, she drifted forward into the commotion, her eyes searching where she'd last seen the telltale hat. There was no way she could check if he had gone into the men's room, so she stood outside the door and continued to search the crowd for him, her mom, and her cat. A tear spilled from her eye.

I love you so much, Plume. I'll never stop looking for you.

But as anxious time passed and Mr. Hamid did not emerge from the men's room, a sudden flush of anxiety hit her. Breathless, she put her head down and sobbed until she heard her mom's voice, shouting.

Looking up she spotted her mother in the crowd, tugging at a tuxedoed man's luggage. Nearby Mr. Hamid stood, issuing commands to the big man in the tux. The man had a square jaw and closely cropped black hair and dressed all in black with a black cap he made a menacing figure. Even his eyes were black, hidden behind sunglasses that shifted as he fought with Mom over the luggage handle.

"Josh, help!" Sara yelled as loudly as she could, hoping her urgency would bring airport security personnel, and then she raced over to help her mother.

"The animal is mine!" Mr. Hamid cried, and joined the tug-of-war over the package, which at closer look was not a suitcase at all but an elaborate, royal-looking pet carrier.

Plume!

Nudging Mr. Hamid, Sara gripped the handle of the cat carrier. "Give me back my kitty!" she hollered.

"No," he said, so close she could feel the heat of his breath. "It is mine."

"It's not an 'it'!" she yelled back in his face. "Plume is a she!" Sara yanked on the pet carrier's handle.

"Now what's going on over here?"

They all turned at the new voice. An official-looking man in dark blue trousers and a light blue V-neck shirt put his hand over all of theirs on the handle of the crate. The security guard was a strong man and others in the same uniform pushed their way through the crowd and surrounded the crate. Sara let go and so did her mom and finally so did Mr. Hamid's assistant.

"Sir," the strong security guard said to Mr. Hamid. "Let go."

Mr. Hamid closed his eyes in disappointment, and then he too released his hold of the crate handle.

Each of the security guards, four in all, pulled them aside individually. The original one took Mr. Hamid away and started questioning him. A lady guard took Mom away, and the biggest guard of all spoke to Mr. Hamid's aide and limo driver, nose to nose.

"What are you all fighting over?" the security guard said to Sara. He was a man in his late twenties, wiry and serious, but with kindly eyes. "What's in the crate? We're required to check it. You might as well give your account...uh, your story."

A rush of emotion swelled in Sara's chest, flushing her face. "My cat is in that man's crate. Her name is Plume, and that guy in the big hat broke into our house and pet-napped her and now he's trying to leave the country. Oh, if I could only hold her now, you'd see." Tears welled and she choked a little. "I miss her so much."

And closing her eyes and cradling her arms, she sobbed, until she heard a mewing sound. She listened over the din of the airport terminal and heard it again. A soft meow, not loud, but striking and distinct as Plume's sweet voice.

"*Moo-row,*" Plume cried again, calling to her. Through her tears, Sara saw the crate that held her precious cat. *That's the key! Plume is mine, and I am Plume's.* Let Plume show everyone whom she belongs to!

Sara rushed past the guard toward the crate where two new guards had assembled. Mr. Hamid saw her running and cut in front of her to reach the crate first. One of the guards figured out how the elaborate padded crate worked and opened the gate, and the occupant did not wait. Plume weaseled past the guard's hands and raced around in a blurring circle.

"What? What is that fluffy-tailed thing?" the guard who had opened the crate exclaimed.

Sara smiled. "That's my kitty, Plume. Here, Plume. Here, Princess." She crouched and held out her arms, hoping Plume would jump into them.

Plume seemed to be avoiding Mr. Hamid who had a security guard tugging on one arm, and he pulled and pulled the guard until finally the empty crate was his. He wheeled around, breaking free of the guard's grasp, and then said loudly so all could hear, "Cat, get back in the crate. Here, kitty, kitty."

Sara was certain Plume would not come when called this way, but then her heart sank when Plume wound through the hustle of people's legs and faced Mr. Hamid, her poofy tail held high. She meowed at Hamid. *She's going to him,* she thought, and the tears came again, and she choked in despair as Hamid smiled and beckoned her cat toward the crate he held. Plume stared into Mr. Hamid's dark eyes, then walked drunkenly toward the door of the crate.

The security guards looked befuddled. The one who had interviewed Mr. Hamid said, "Put your cat back in its crate, Mr. Hamid, or we'll do it for you."

And the security guards think she's Mr. Hamid's cat, Sara brooded. She wiped her face and decided to give it another try.

"Plume?" Sara said, approaching her cat, who cocked her head and stared at Mr. Hamid.

"Plume?" she cried again.

The cat did not turn with that owl-like crane of the neck that cats often exhibit. Her tail shot down and she trotted, low to the ground, and then sprang with a *hissssss—*

Mr. Hamid reacted to the quickness with a frightened shriek and his hand came up, too late—

Plume clung to his shoulder, and then getting her paws set, hopped up onto the top of his hat. There, she kicked her hind legs out and wheeled, swinging down to swat at Mr. Hamid's face. As the hat collapsed, the cat sank and clung to the side of his head. Plume bit Mr. Hamid's ear.

"Ow! Stupid animal!" Orkhan Hamid bellowed in pain and then flung the cat to the floor. Plume landed on her feet, but she'd taken Mr. Hamid's hat with her; all of it. The tall hat lay on the floor, dented and crumpled.

Plume looked around, then meowed in the voice of a young lady cat who is no longer a kitten.

Mr. Hamid's personal valet lunged for Plume, but Plume was too fast, too low, too slippery, and the big man didn't even get a finger on her as she raced around the onlookers and then sat, farther away, her shoulders upright, her yellow eyes searching for threat.

She moved closer to me, Sara thought and sank into a crouch. "Come here, kitty. Princess Plume? Show everybody whose baby you are?"

Plume trotted to her, sniffed her hand, and then her tail came up again, fluffy and proud, and she meowed and purred.

The limo driver rushed them, and Josh stepped in front of him, taking the brunt force of the hit and fell to the ground. This drew the entire security team who seized Mr. Hamid's assistant and pulled him away. Sara heard the door to the security detainment room close, and then she looked back toward Plume.

Plume sniffed her hand again, and then wheeled and tickled Sara's nose with the tip of her tail. Flushed with joy, she picked up her cat. To the nearest security guard, she said, "This is my cat. That man in the funny hat broke into my house and stole her."

"All right," the security guard said, raising his hands. He squinted skeptically. "I think we've seen enough." He whirled and said, "Team, let's take all of them in the back and get this settled. See who really owns Fluffy."

To Sara's surprise, Mom stepped forward. "I can prove who owns that cat." From her purse, Mom pulled out a folded-up document.

Mrs. Massey said, "Take a look. It says we own this cat, one-year-old, neutered female...and the cat's markings are described right here." Mom tapped her finger on the document.

The security guard turned to Mr. Hamid. "Sir, what do you have to say to these charges? Did you steal their cat and try to leave the country?"

They all looked at Mr. Hamid, and he scowled and shook his head. No one watching said a word, though in the distance Sara could hear the voice over the terminal PA system; the first call for boarding on the flight her mother had booked them on.

They'd done all this for a cat, a cat that made a difference in people's lives. Mr. Hamid had been willing to steal for this cat and what it could do. Sara felt a pang of sympathy for the man. Striding toward him, Plume in her arms, she even considered giving him the cat, knowing that giving was a blessing too, but the Turk held up his hand and cleared his throat, and even wiped away a tear of his own.

To those crowded around and listening, he said, "I am embarrassed to say that the feline has spoken. It— or, she, as the girl said—has told and taught me something today. The animal is no longer mine. I can feel it, from the prick of the cat's developing claws. It has made its message clear. It is no longer mine, nor my family's precious possession." He paused to pick his hat off the floor, and straightened it and put it back on his head. Arranging the linen layers that comprised the hat, he stood up straight and then bowed to Sara.

"You see," he continued, "this cat is the one, with all the characteristics of the bloodline my sultan family prized for centuries, since it was written about Lake Van and the flood." He took a breath and Sara could see the pain in the man's expression. Mr. Hamid was certainly passionate about his cats, even if he called them "its."

"Mr. Hamid, I'd like you to—" she started. He cut her off. "No, Sara. It is you who must take the cat." His once hypnotizing eyes now revealed another side to the man: sincerity and a sad longing for something he knew was no longer his or meant to be. "I used to believe this cat was my right, my possession, but you and the cat have taught me something. It belongs to you, and you to it."

The Turk bowed again and motioned to his aide, whom, by good fortune, the arresting security agents had just released. "Come, Harry, we can still catch the flight."

"Mr. Hamid!" Sara shouted.

He stopped and looked at her, sadness on his face.

Sara stared down at the ground, though the man's desperate eyes no longer hypnotized, and thought about what she wanted to say. With a stammer she said, "What will you do back in Turkey, Mr. Hamid? Will you be all right?"

"I will do my best," he answered, leaning toward the gate. "I just know that the cat gave me many answers while it was clawing and biting my ear." Reaching up, he touched his ear as he looked at Plume in Sara's arms.

"It told me that I may have power in my small kingdom back in Turkey only through gentleness, not through force. Through granting freedom and independence, not by rigid control. The cat belongs to you, Sara Massey." And with that, Orkhan Hamid, the self-proclaimed great-great-grandson of Turkish Sultans, bowed to Sara and her cat, and then he and his chauffeur gave their boarding passes to the airline official and disappeared from sight.

Mom came over and hugged her. Sara squeezed Plume and kissed her cat on the furry head. Spotting the ornate cat carrier that Mr. Hamid had left behind, she stashed Plume inside, safe and secure.

"This last part's up to me," Josh said, and he went to work on the person at the counter to try to get them their money back for the unused tickets.

Chapter Twenty-Three

The summer flew by as it always does for the children who enjoy it so much. Seventh grade started, and in Spanish class, Sara asked Donna, "How are you, friend?" in Spanish.

"Por favor. Muchas gracias," Donna answered.

Zoe joining them, the three of them walked the halls together after class, preparing for the final stretch of the day. For Sara it was just language arts, history, and then the weekend. She smiled but stopped when out of the corner of her vision she saw a scuffle. By the lockers, sixth-grader Bess Banazak had shoved little Nelly Nythers against a locker door and was telling her something while balling her fists under the girl's collar.

"Come on, girls," Sara said, leading Donna and Zoe to the two sixth graders. Bess towered over Nelly, and Sara could hear her angry words now. "You don't make me look bad or I'll—"

"Or you will what?" Sara said with authority.

Big Bess glanced back and eyed Sara, then Donna, who was taller than her.

"Seventh graders on patrol for bullying," Donna said.

Zoe stepped up, smiled, and added, "Get going, Bess, or we'll report you. All three of us."

Bess's face paled, and she kept her head down as she scurried away, toward the girl's bathroom.

"Thank you," a still-shaken Nelly said. She flipped her curls aside and started off...

"Nelly, wait!" Sara called. Nelly turned. "Your hair..." Sara paused only to realize the poor girl was probably bracing herself for an insult. She'd been through such teasing herself. "You have pretty hair," Sara said and gave the girl a smile.

History class was fun and she went home in a great mood. The bus ride continued the innocent frolicking. They even played the baby game of *rock, paper, scissors* until the old bus driver stopped the bus and told them to be quiet, he couldn't concentrate on driving the bus when they were so noisy.

She got off the bus laughing, let herself in the front, and left her stuff from school in the kitchen. In the bathroom she scrubbed and dried her hands thoroughly and then went into her bedroom.

"I can't bring scents from school that kitty princess might not like on her fur," she said to the cat on the bed. Then, she scooped Plume up, and the cat twisted her head in that owl-like way and stared at her with her yellow eyes. With Plume in her arms, Sara opened the door to the hall. She moved around the corner and then gave a start and almost tripped. Lincoln had surprised them, and Plume clawed at Sara's shoulder, forcing her to release her. Plume landed on her feet and sniffed Lincoln. The collie sniffed the cat and then tried to sniff all of the cat, and Plume pawed the dog's nose away from her fluffy tail.

Catching her breath, Sara said, "Link, I don't think Princess Plume would like your doggie breath on her precious fur."

Plume pawed the collie's nose again and then strode away, her poofy, feathery tail held high as she vanished back into the bedroom. Stunned, Sara glanced at the always-hungry dog and then back at the crack where she'd left her bedroom door open. She blurted out laughing and continued to do so as she fed Lincoln and then readied and served a dish of turkey stew cat food to the Turkish princess cat who had turned her life around.

Acknowledgments

I would like to thank the following people for their assistance with the research and publication of this novel.

Lisa Scullard and Amy Newman for their insight into gymnastics practices and tournaments. Any mistakes in the following tale are my own.

Karen and Maya Lombardo for their encouragement and feedback, and Lynn Hickey for her soul support.

And finally I'd like to thank Kay and Steve Moore for entrusting me with the inspiration for this novel, a wild kitten.

About the Author

Dean Lombardo is the author of four novels, including Donkey Sense and Princess Plume, both Clean Reads publications. A Connecticut native, Dean now lives in Northern Virginia with his wife, two teenagers, and a dog and cat.

CPSIA information can be obtained
at www.ICGtesting.com
Printed in the USA
LVOW12s0109080817
544194LV00002B/478/P